Saving the Second Kingdom

Kingdom Warriors of
the Seven Mountains Series

Kim Jennings

A catalogue record for this book is available from the National Library of Australia

This book is, of course, fiction.

Publisher:
Australian Self Publishing Group, Pty. Ltd / Inspiring Publishers
PO Box 159, Calwell, ACT 2905, Australia.
Phone: 61-(0) 2 6291-2904
http://australianselfpublishinggroup.com

National Library of Australia Prepublication Data Service

Author: Kim Jennings

Title: **Saving the Second Kingdom:**
Kingdom Warriors of the seven mountains Series

ISBN: 978-1-923087-09-5 (print)
978-1-923087-08-8 (PDF eBook)
978-1-923087-07-1 (ePub2)

This book is dedicated to

Yeshua Hamashiach

Acknowledgements

My sincere thanks to my Husband Jonathan and my Daughter Katelyn for all their help and input into this book. Without their support and typing skills I could not have done this.

I would like to acknowledge the following people for their influence on my journey.

Paul Smith, My brother for his endless counsel
Book of Isaiah- passion Version
Steve Shultz @ Elijah Streams
Johnny Enlow @ restor.7
Robin D Bullock @ eleventh hour
Kat Kerr @ katkerr.com
Amanda Grace @ Ark of grace Ministries
Col Stringer- 800 Horsemen
Lana Vawser @ lanavawers.com
Tim Sheets- Oasis Church
Tiffany Root and kirk VandeGuchte- Seeking the glory of God

Contents

Chapter One
The Rising Sun

A ray of light pierced through the crack in the curtains devouring the darkness in its path. Orchestrating the sweet sound of the morning choir.

Vicky sat up in bed, yawning and stretching. Rubbing her big blue eyes, she stumbled out of bed and made her way to the bathroom to splash her face with cold water. Looking out of the bathroom window she could see the horses had already been let out of the stables.

Oh no, I'm late! She thought to herself as she quickly ran back to her room and got dressed into her usual jeans and a t-shirt. With one boot on, hopping down the hall towards the front door struggling with the other, she heard her mother call out, "Vicki, don't forget to eat something. I'm sure Lynda can wait five more minutes."

Vicki quickly ran up the hall to her mother in the kitchen. She grabbed a banana and turned to run back out.

"That's not enough," argued her mother, but Vicki already halfway down the hall again yelled back, "No it's fine, Mum! It's all I feel like – I'll have lunch at school."

With that, she ran outside and down the laneway leading to the stables next to her Cousin Lynda's house.

Vicky and her mother had come to live with Lynda, Vicki's cousin on her father's side, on the beautiful, lush 200 acre cattle stud called 'Cooinda' an Aboriginal word meaning 'all welcome'. Nestled in the valleys and hills of the mighty Darling Down mountain ranges- the Darling Down tablelands.

Vicki's father, Charles, was an officer in the Australian Army as was his father before him all the way back to his great, great grandfather who served as an officer in the Light Horse Regiment of World War I. He was part of the famous 800 in the Charge of Beersheba in October of 1917. A renowned horseman that passed on his horsemanship skills

down through the generations and Charles was no exception. Sadly though, Charles had been killed in action during his last deployment four years prior.

Vicki's mother, Veronica, couldn't afford to keep their farm on the small widow's pension she received, so Lynda – a widow herself – offered Vonnie and Vicki to come live in the small caretaker's cottage in return for looking after Cooinda when she went away on her frequent business trips.

Vicki looked after the two horses, Gisselle and old Dude. In return she was allowed to ride them and treat them as her own. She was very grateful to Lynda for the opportunity as horses were her first love: it was in her blood. Horses were all she ever thought about and working with them helped her through the grief of losing her father.

She really loved living at Cooinda, however when she was alone sometimes Vicki wished she could have a dog to keep her company and be her friend but she felt her mother had enough on her plate already.

Saving the Second Kingdom

So Vicki never asked for a puppy as she did not want to put any more burdens on her mother.

"Vicki, I've let the horses out and un-rugged them, but I haven't given them their hay yet. Can you feed up and muck out please?" called Lynda from the window.

"Yeah, sure!" Vicki yelled back and hurried along to the feed-shed to get the hay. Vicki loved caring for the horses as much as she did riding them. To her, It was all a labour of love and gave her so much enjoyment – even mucking out the stables.

After tending to the horses, Vicki hurried to get ready for school and walked down to meet the school bus.

There had been a lot of talk about a new sickness spreading across the world, and the small town was buzzing with gossip. Rumours were going around the school, but Vicki took it as just that: gossip brought on by fear. In her mind it was simple, if it really was as bad as they say, and if governments really wanted to stop the spread, wouldn't they close airports to international flights?

Instead, people were still flying all around the world even from infected countries, so either it was not as bad as people said, or the governments were deliberately allowing it to spread. Why would they do that? This was just logical in her mind, so she put most of it down to news reports spreading fear as they tend to.

Life carried on normally in the little town. News of the sickness continued and soon it was pronounced a pandemic. Announcements went out all over that schools and most workplaces would close. Everyone was asked to keep travel to a minimum only making necessary trips, to distance themselves from others and to wear a mask. They called it lockdown. Vicki believed it all could have been avoided in the first place and deemed the social distancing absurd.

Vicki wondered how it would affect her and her best friend Yarran, as they were both sixteen and had decided that it was to be their last year in school as they both wanted to pursue careers with horses.

Yarran was from a very well-known Aboriginal family famous in the area as the best horse breakers in the district. He and his father had spent the last ten years fighting against the wicked agenda of the Government to cull all brumbies and poison all dingos in the area. They have been catching the wild brumbies of the tablelands and turning them into wonderful stockhorses to save them from the cruel culling. As well as removing as many poison baits as they could find, meant for the dingos in the area. The government was hiring people to lay poison down but many other animals were being killed too. Much to their horror they had also found that someone else was poisoning the local drinking holes for wildlife. Sadly they had found many different animals fallen prey to this and many were brumby's.

Yarran wanted to help his father full-time and shine a spotlight on just how excellent the brumbies could be when handled right. Many even made much-loved children's horses. His plan was to start entering in all the local stockhorse competitions and then go state-wide.

Life with the lockdowns didn't change too much for Vicki, it felt like an extended holiday. She had lots of time to spend with the horses and in the kitchen garden helping her mother out.

As the weeks rolled by, Vicki started to notice that the sky was always cloudy: dark and gloomy. She had to think hard to remember when the last sunny day was. As far as the eye could see, there were no blue skies to be seen.

It was strange, Vicki had never seen the sky like this before, yet most people didn't seem to notice unless it she pointed it out to them. Still, they acted as if it was normal, or they would blame it on global warming, which was another thing that didn't make sense to Vicki. She had written an essay on global warming for school and the consensus from the majority of scientists was they discounted it as a myth. Their figures were very different Indeed.

The garden and the native flowers that usually flourished that time of year seemed struggling to bloom and the vegetables were not growing well at all. The clouds seemed to be filtering out the sunlight. Vicki brought it up with her mother and Lynda, but they told her she was being ridiculous and that she was reading too much into it. They suggested she did more work to keep her over-active mind busy.

Vicki rolled her eyes at this suggestion and instead went to saddle up Gisselle, she decided to go for a ride to her favourite place in the whole district: the creek flats in the foothills of Mount Yarramundi. A huge mountain, the tallest in the entire tablelands. It loomed over the town and surrounding farmlands consuming the horizon.

She had no sooner ridden through the front gate and onto the side of the road when the sound of a big V8 engine broke through the silence, and a white ute came into view. As it drew closer, Vicki couldn't help but admire it. She had never seen such a nice ute before. Its motor purred as it glided along the road. It was pearl white, and it had an electric blue lightning bolt down the bonnet that branched out down both sides. It reached around to the tailgate spelling 'Striker'. The ute was marvellous; the lightning seemed to shift with the change of light and made it look alive. The final touch was 'ANGEL' as the licence plates.

The driver slowed to pass Vicki and Gisselle and came to a stop at the side of the road. The dark tinted window rolled down and a man's head peeked out.

"Hi, I hope I didn't frighten your horse. I'm sorry to bother you, but I think I'm a little lost. Could you please just point me in the right direction?" He asked.

All the stories of 'stranger danger' Vicki heard as a young child sprang to the forefront of her mind in that moment. She cautiously pushed Gisselle to go a little closer for ease of conversation, but she stayed alert and out of reach.

"Where are you trying to get to?" She questioned.

"Well, I am looking for a field called 'Mount Yarramundi Creek Flats'." The man answered.

"Really!" Vicki said surprised. "I'm just riding out there now actually."

"Oh huh, small world," said the driver.

"It's super easy to find by road," explained Vicki, "you just follow this road until you see the National Park sign saying 'Mount Yarramundi

Road' on your right. Turn down that road, follow the signs, and you will come to a gravel road. Go a little further till the land opens up to a beautiful tree-lined field, and you are there." She pointed the way.

"Thank you so much! I was thinking I'd taken a wrong turn somewhere. Hey, by the way, just so you know I'm going to meet my team there. We are putting up a big tent and will be holding some meetings there over the next few weeks for all the locals. We are hoping to bring some light into these dark times. Why don't you bring your family or friends, and come check it out?"

"Here is a pamphlet so you know it's legit. I am an Evangelist, and I travel around going about my Father's business." He added as he held out the pamphlet for Vicki to take. She reached down and took it, his words about the light and darkness spoke to her.

No sooner had she started to read the pamphlet when a second voice came from inside the car and spoke, "Whoever walks in the darkness does not know where they are going."

Vicki laughed as it was clearly the voice of a parrot, but still she couldn't shake the words of light and darkness 'again!'

"That's so strange." She said to the man, "I keep seeing the dark clouds in the sky but no one else seems to notice them." She said in amazement of what the parrot had just said to her.

"I'm sorry, that is my side kick, and he often has too much to say for himself." The man said trying to comfort her. Vicki laughed,

"Would you like to meet him?" he asked. Vicki gingerly nodded her head grinning. She loved birds.

She jumped down from Gisselle and moved off the road. The door slowly opened and out hopped a middle aged man wearing a surfing Homer Simpson Hawaiian shirt, white shorts and very loud sponge bob square pants socks with joggers. Vicki couldn't help but to laugh a little. On his shoulder was the most stunning blue and gold Macaw parrot. This was the first one Vicki had ever seen in real life "Oh, he is beautiful!!" she exclaimed, "I never realised how big they are, Wow."

The man walked over and put his hand out saying "My name is Paul, it's nice to meet you and this is my bestie, Word" he added"

"Hi I'm Vicki, "she said shaking his hand, "Word, that is different, why word?" she asked.

"Well my Father has a great book of truth, it's a guide book for a life walking in the Light. It's referred to as the word, and my feathery friend Word here knows every verse in it. He loves to quote it for people. He has a gift of seeing into a person's heart and knowing just which verses a person needs to hear."

"The day my Father gave me the mantle of Evangelist, he gifted me Word and my ute, 'Striker', If you look closely at Word's wings when he stretches them out you will see my Father's sense of humour, Word also has lightning bolts on his wings," Paul exclaimed.

"Oh, I get it, lightning strike, 'Striker', and 'Word' because he gives people words to help, I love that, it's very cool" Laughed Vicki.

"So it sounds to me, Vicki that you are awake and you are struggling to make sense of what is going on in the word!" Paul interjected as they gave Word a scratch.

"Awake? I'm not sure I understand what you mean" asked Vicki puzzled, did he think she was sleeping?

"Well I mean like, you can see the darkness that blankets the earth like thick clouds that cover the Nations, when no one else seems to see. It's like they are in a slumber. Vicki that's great you are awake, that's what my mission is, to go around this Nation waking people up.

I really think you should come tonight, I think you will get a lot out of the meeting, I think we were meant to meet here today. I'll teach you all about The Father and The King that are being hidden from you. You will meet other like-minded people that are also awake. The first meeting will be 7pm tonight till maybe 9pm. come along bring anyone you like, you know where it is ha-ha-ha" Paul got back into his ute.

His words resonated in Vicki and what King is he talking about? Vicki though to herself as she climbed back into the saddle. Paul started the ute and said "It was really good meeting you Vicki, hope I see you again." Vicki agreed. In that moment she decided to ride over to Yarran's place and tell him all about Paul and what he had said as Yarran also was 'awake' as Paul had put it.

When she found Yarran, she told him all about her chance meeting with Paul and they both agreed to meet up at the creek flats at 7pm to go to this 'meeting' and see what it's all about.

7pm came around, Vicki and Yarran arrived like clockwork. They were curious and excited to learn of a King and hoped for some answers finally about what is going on.

The tent was big, it could seat a couple of hundred people easily and beside it was a smaller tent with a sign saying 'Alanah's Café' with tables and chairs set up out of the front.

As they approached the main entrance, a lady greeted them, "Hi, I am Alanah, so glad you came, where would you like to sit?" Vicki barely had time to say "Hi" when Paul and a man with a guitar over his shoulder appeared.

"Vicki, you came and you brought a friend, oh I'm so glad." Said Paul

"Yes hi, this is my friend Yarran. Yarran this is Paul" Vicki replied as Yarran shook Paul's hand.

"I see you have met Alanah, this is Ethan. He is an anointed guitarist. He writes Kingdom worship music that is very powerful, you guys will love it!" said Paul.

Vicki and Yarran smiled at Ethan, Vicki was a little shy of him. Then she noticed the back of Ethan's guitar had the same kind of lightning bolt that Paul's ute, Striker has, with branches spreading all over the back of the guitar and reaching around to the front. It was alive with colour that flashed and changed as it moved in the light. The branches stretched all the way up the front of the neck (of the guitar) to form the word 'Passion' on the headstock. It was very ornate and beautiful.

"Wow! That is the coolest guitar I have ever seen" said Vicki, "Yeah same here" added Yarran.

"Why thank you, it was a gift from my Father." Ethan replied "you two should come sit up the front of the stage, it looks even better under the lights." He added. Paul agreed and ushered them both to the same vacant seats right in front of the stage.

   Saving the Second Kingdom

The meeting got underway and Paul taught on some incredible topics. He explained that there are five spiritual Kingdoms, the first being 'The Father's Kingdom and our real home', It is now ruled by Father's son, The King. This is his reward for fighting a great battle to win us back to the Father at much cost to Himself because in the very beginning when the first of mankind walked the earth, we became separated from The Father by an enemy. Now, thanks to The King's supreme sacrifice we have a way back to the Father.

Hearing of The Kings great sacrifice touched both Vicki and Yarran's hearts. Something in them just knew these words were true.

Next Paul taught that the Kingdom of Man was governed by seven Mountains. The five Kingdoms and seven mountains were a little confusing for Vicki and Yarran. But they did their best to follow along and tried to take in as much as they could.

At the end of the meeting Paul called for anyone who would like to be welcomed back 'into' their true family, to come up the front and pledge their allegiance to The Father by acknowledging The Kings sacrifice for them and surrendering their hearts to Him. In so doing, joining The King in the ongoing fight of the good fight for righteousness upon the Earth.

Vicki and Yarran, so grateful The Almighty Deity would love them so much, He would suffer the worst punishment imaginable just to give them a way to get home to the Father's Kingdom. They felt a strong pull on their hearts to go up to the front and receive The King and meet their real Father for the very first time and so they did.

When the meeting was over, Vicki and Yarran headed over to the café and ordered two coffees. They both sat and were in a deep discussion about all they had just learned and what they experienced when they went to receive The King. They found they both had similar things happened to them but they could not explain it. It was like they were drunk but they did not drink. They were laughing uncontrollably yet there was nothing funny.

Eventually Paul and Ethan meandered over and sat with Vicki and Yarran, Alanah brought out everyone's coffee and sat down as well.

Paul could see that there was something special about these two simple country teens. He knew The Father had a calling for them. He asked if they had enjoyed the meeting and both Vicki and Yarran were full of enthusiasm, talking very fast about what they had each experienced when they went to receive The King into their hearts.

Paul, Ethan and Alanah laughed, Alanah, gestured with her hands for them to slow down saying, "We can't understand you, but we love your excitement."

Vicki tried to explain as best she could, "When we went up the front and invited The King into our hearts, something happened to us, "she went on, "We were filled with this amazing feeling, it was like electricity, we felt tingly all over and then our legs went all wobbly, we couldn't walk straight, all we could do was laugh uncontrollably, we laughed for so long, we couldn't stop and the tingly feeling just go stronger and stronger." She said wide eyed.

"Yeah it was awesome" Yarran added, "I feel so light, like air. We both feel different" he said.

"Oh that's so fantastic guys, it is amazing isn't it! That was Lord Sabaoth, he is the third member of The Kingdom Head and he will dwell inside you to guide you, speak to you and give you many spiritual gifts. He also brings the Glory, which you got a little sample of tonight" Paul explained.

Vicki and Yarran were astounded, they knew they found something real and powerful that offered real answers to all of their questions. It was like a light shining through the darkness and best of all, they were not alone anymore.

Chapter Two
The Great Falling Away

The weeks rolled into months, it felt like forever ago since Vicki went to Paul's tent meeting or even saw Yarran, and lockdown seemed to be a never ending scenario.

The sky seemed even gloomier bit by bit, day by day, with dark clouds looming overhead and lightning strikes starting bush fires everywhere.

Vonnie and Lynda were still not 'awake', every time Vicki tried to speak to them about the darkness or about their real Father, they would shut her down with the same argument. That she had an over active mind and read too much into things.

Vicki withdrew to her room, since accepting The King. Vicki had tried to spend time everyday just talking quietly to him on her bed and asking him to open the eyes of her mother and cousin.

Looking out of her bedroom window, seeing how dark things had become. She felt her sprit rise up inside her until she cried out to The Father. "Why is this happening? How did it get so bad??"

"There must be something we can do!" she cried.

Then, Vicki felt a change in the air, there was a shift in the atmosphere and her room filled with a misty cloud. Vicki began to feel as she did the night of the tent meeting.

A great white light appeared in the centre of the room, it got brighter and brighter until there in front of her stood the figure of a man.

The white light was so bright it was hard to make out any detail at first but as light gradually faded, more detail was revealed. Until standing before her was a man, dressed in kingly robes with a beautiful crown adorned with sparkling gems of all colours.

Vicki was a little in shock but because there was such an overwhelming feeling of peace and love that engulfed her, she knew it was ok. Something inside her told her this was The King, sent by the Father.

As the kingly figure moved towards her, he reassured her saying "Don't be afraid my child. I have heard your cries and have come to give answers to your questions and reveal my destiny I have for your life. I have much to teach you if you will allow me?"

Vicki was barely able to draw breath but she managed to reply "Yes of Course."

"What I have to tell you will be revelation to your spirit child, as up until now everything you have known has been a great deception, to keep all of my children from really knowing me and walking in their true destiny."

"My child, I am The King of All Kingdoms, The King of kings, I am the light of the world, I am pure love and I rule over all things!"

"I have many sons and daughters, you child are my beloved daughter, to whom I have given much, you are more precious to me than all of creation itself. As are all of my children, each one I named and planned out a destiny for. I equipped each with all the special gifts they would require to reach their destiny. I anointed each one with my love and blessings all before they were even born, that you all should carry my authority and have dominion over all the Earth, and the other Kingdoms.

The darkness you see now blanketing your nation, is because of the evil king and his army. The very one I defeated long ago.

He once had much power and was a very great leader in his kingdom. One day he saw that I was planning something new on the Earth, a new kingdom, a kingdom for my children. The Kingdom of Man.

He saw that this kingdom would have more power than his own and this made the evil king very mad indeed. He came into my kingdom and he waged war against Me and my army of Hosts. He swore to himself that he would rule from High places, that he would be as man is with dominion over all.

You see my child these were the five spiritual Kingdoms of old, before I created mankind- 1 My Kingdom, 2 Angelic Kingdom, 3 Animal Kingdom, 4 Plant Kingdom and 5 The Earth Kingdom (dirt).

I laid down in the Earth Kingdom and left my impression in the dirt, then I spoke man into that impression and then I breathed my spirit into him so he would have life. This created a shift in the order of Kingdoms, the kingdom of dirt was now the kingdom of man. So now the five kingdoms to this day are, 1 The Father's Kingdom, 2 Man's Kingdom, 3 Angelic Kingdom, 4 Animal Kingdom and 5 the Plant Kingdom.

This is why the evil one was so outraged, he wanted his kingdom to be second, to be my family. But my family had to come from my image. He refused to acknowledge that there was now a new kingdom with greater authority than his own.

Refusing to bow to me and banished from his own kingdom in disgrace along with his fallen army, he designed a plan, long ago to steal each and every identity of my children preventing them from reaching their destinies and stewarding the earth as they were created to do. Forever separating me from my children. "Ha-ha-ha, or so he thought "added the King.

He desires the power you have been blessed with through my inheritance for you.

Though he himself can never possess your power, he can access it by deceiving my children into agreement with him and leading them into his wicked plans. He often disguises his wicked agendas making them seem harmless or for the 'greater good'. Often labelled with 'global'.

This is why the world is in the dismay you see around you. The evil one flips the things that I have set in place to be good and bring joy, into being things that bring devastation, death and destruction. What you see around you right now is creation moaning and travailing for my sons and daughters to be awakened to the truth and in their true authority, steward all of creation and put the world back as it was meant to be!!"

Vicki pondered this for a minute "But if you are The King of 'All', higher than the evil king, why can't you just stop him" she asked curiously.

"Well, you see The Father gifted all of his children with free will. He will not take your choice away, He Is a true gentleman. He allows his children the right to choose even if it is not what He wants for you. He did give man a guide book to help them find my light, and to live by His laws.

The Father is pure love, he cannot abide sin, knowing this The evil one tricked my very first born son of mankind, long ago in the ancient days, into making a choice that caused the curse of sin to befall the earth and thus separating my Father from His children 'forever,' or so the evil one thought but Father had a plan from the very beginning as he foresaw this happening.

   Saving the Second Kingdom

Father spoke his word into flesh and I came to live among you."

"I fought a great battle just like my messenger Paul had told you about the night of the tent meeting. I defeated that old snake, the king of the earth, and by doing so, I created a way back to The Father for all of his children."

The King took off his outer robe and began to pull a chair over from in front of Vicki's desk, in the far corner of her room. It was then that she noticed scars on his hands- holes that went straight through them. As his tunic and long, brown hair slid to one side of his back with his movements, she saw many scars at the top of his back that looked like stripes, as though he had been whipped!

He surely must have been in a great battle," thought Vicki, he must love us all so much to suffer like that just to give us a way home back to Father and freedom. She solemnly thought to herself. In that instant The King looked at her with tears pooling in his eyes and said "Oh my darling daughter, if only you could know how much I love you. I would happily give myself over to be sacrificed again, just to save one of my precious lambs."

When The King spoke these words, a feeling started to rise up inside of Vicki, the likes of which she had never felt. Tears welled in her eyes as she felt the truth of his words piece her very soul and as his love washed over her, she wept.

"That is My Holy Spirit that you are feeling, 'Lord Sabaoth' "The King interjected, "My spirit shall dwell in your heart, and will always guide you to know my truth and my voice daughter. He will lead you and give you wisdom to know when the evil one is trying to deceive you. Always listen and be led by my spirit from now on."

"I will Lord, I will always follow your leading." She said as she wept with tears of truth.

Chapter Three
Mountain Mandate

"**F**ather what can I do to help you in this war? I want to fight the evil king and his army with you." Exclaimed Vicki

"Ha- ha -ha" The King laughed with a roar from his belly. "I love your eager spirit my little one, you are my delight!" he proclaimed with such love in his voice.

"I will tell you about the seven mountains through which this world is ruled." Said The King he went on,

"Earth is an image of my Kingdom. In my Kingdom there are seven spirits of the Father, and those seven spirits are reflected here on earth as Spiritual Mountains that I have put in place for my children to rule and reign over, that is my commandment for you all. I anointed all of you with the gifts you will need to operate in which ever mountain is your destiny. These mountains are, The Mountains of Government, Media, Arts and Entertainment, Economy, Family, Religion and Education." The King explained.

Then he looked directly into Vicki's eyes and with a note of seriousness he said "It is on these mountains that my children 'MUST' take a stand and win them back as the enemy has taken control of all seven of them. I need my children to proclaim them back from the enemy and usher in a new age. The likes of which, has never been seen on earth before."

Vicki sat wide eyed glued to every word The King spoke. Her spirit was hungry to know more and her heart was eager to fight the good fight.

"This is why the world is so dark right now" said The King. "In my word this is written as the time when darkness blankets the earth and everything that is good is called evil and what is evil is called good my child."

"I have a destiny for you Vicki, if you will walk in it. I will use you to do great things in my nations. You will be a Prophetess for the seven mountains in the nations, you will be my warrior prophetess."

Vicki was honoured that her Father had that much trust in her but the title 'Warrior Prophetess of the seven mountains' was very daunting. How could a sixteen year old girl accomplish much at all.

Upon having these thoughts in her mind, The King responded to them as if she had spoken them out loud.

"Do not fear child, fear is a spirit and it cancels out faith. I will be with you, I am always with you and it is only through My Spirit, Lord Sabaoth that you can do anything required of you." Then he went on.

"My child I am gifting you some Kingdom weapons fit for a Kingdom warrior- My Armour and my army."

"The first of which I will give you is my Belt of Truth. By wearing this every day you hold My truth close and allow it to surround you."

The King held out his hand to Vicki and there in his hand was a beautiful ornate leather belt, which had words and scrolls etched into it all over. As he opened his hand further, is seemed to come to life and snaked its way over to Vicki and wrapped itself around her waist, even going through the belt loops on her jeans. It buckled itself up to a perfect fit.

Vicki sat wide eyed, mouth open and frozen, she did not know what had just happened.

"Fear Not!" said The King, his words seemed to penetrate her very spirit and instantly she felt peace.

"The second weapon I give you is the sword of My spirit," and just like that the most beautiful sword appeared in The Kings hands. With beautifully decorated handle and scabbard. Studded with gems of every colour and shape and beautiful etchings of scrolls. He held his hands outstretched towards Vicki, prompting her to take the sword. She very carefully went to take up the sword, her eyes examining every inch of the perfectly decorated hilt, handle and scabbard.

"Wear this always child" instructed The King.

Excitedly, she took the sword into her hands and attached it to her belt. When something unexpected happened. The sword began to vanish and as it did so a flurry of words began to appear in the air, the words that were etched into the sword. They were lit up, around and around they went like a carousel made of mist. Then they travelled up in front of Vicki and into her heart.

Puzzled and trying not to be afraid, she glanced over at The King who instantly reassured her. "It's OK child, the words you saw are the words of my spirit that now reside in you."

"Now your words have the power of my light, of life and death. So you must learn how to wield them wisely as they are my spiritual swords against the enemy."

"Whenever you need to wield your sword against the enemy, all you have to do is to speak out and decree it and believe!" He emphasised.

"Decrees!!! What are they Lord, I'm not sure?" Vicki asked.

"Well child," said The King in a soft voice, "when one of my children decree something you are making a law, an official order that has the full force of My Kingdom's laws. You can decree to stop something from happening or you may need to decree to make something happen. As long as your decrees line up with my laws it will be done." The King went on…

"You are the daughter of The King most High, your decrees shall carry All the weight of my authority. This is your Kingdom inheritance that I have provided to all of my children."

"When you make your decree, give the assignment to my Army of Hosts which I have assigned to you. They will depart instantly to carry out your order. As your words of decree leave your moth they will become anointed spiritual swords for my Hosts to take up arms against the enemy!"

Then a helmet appeared in The Kings hand. It looked like something a Knight would wear. Beautifully polished like fine silver "Try this on child" prompted The King "This is the helmet of salvation, wear it always, it is a sign to the evil ones that you are my daughter and you operate in my full authority."

Vicki reached out to take the helmet, thinking it would be heavy, she braced herself for the weight but, as she touched it, the helmet turned into a felt hat and not just any felt hat. It was a slouch hat, a real genuine slouch hat, complete with leather band and the rising sun badge. The exact one her great, great, great, grandfather would have worn as part of the uniform in the Australian Light Horse Regiment.

Vicki loved this as it directly connected her to her family history. She noticed though that it was missing the feather. Slouch hats were famous for having a very distinct plume from an emu instead of a normal feather.

The King knew what Vicki was wondering, "The plume will come later child" He said. Vicki felt a little sorry that she had doubted him and she eagerly put the hat on, it was a perfect fit.

"Now for your body armour" proclaimed The King, Vicki's eyes grew wide as she gulped, what will this be she wondered.

"HA -ha-ha" The King laughed at her reaction and put out his hand, there was a rush of wind in his hands which turned into a breastplate. Much like the helmet, it was something a Knight of old would wear. Vicki wondered what this would turn out to be as she reached to take it from The King's hands, now completely trusting in her Father and The King.

As she did so, the breastplate turned back into a gush of wind, like a little whirlwind and danced it's way over to Vicki until it was in front of her, then it grew a bit larger and engulfed Vicki. It swirled around her and then stopped. When Vicki looked down, she was wearing a new T-Shirt of her most favourite colour of all, a beautiful bright blue.

"This is my breastplate of righteousness" Explained the King, "It will protect your heart against doing wrong and against attacks from the enemy."

Vicky was speechless, she was in awe.

The King reached down at his side and pulled up a pair of armoured boots. Again, the kind a Knight would wear, polished to perfection to match the helmet and breastplate.

"These are my shoes of peace" said The King, "They will keep you in readiness. They will make it easy for you to stay calm and trust in me when things go wrong or you are afraid."

Vicki took them from The King, and as she did so they turned into a pair of leather riding boots. Something Vicki was in desperate need of as her old ones were very worn out and a little too small. These new boots fitted like a dream. Vicki was so happy, tears welled up in her eyes. When she looked back at The King to thank him, Sitting in his place was The Father, she rushed to her loving Father's arms and hugged him as she thanked him.

Saving the Second Kingdom

Her Father gently spoke in Vicki's ear as a tear of joy rolled down His cheek. "No my beautiful daughter, thank you for placing your love and trust in me. So many of my children are still lost to me. That I can bless and protect you, makes you even more precious to me." He whispered as he wiped the tear from his cheek with his finger.

"The best is yet to come my child come, let's walk outside, but before we do, there is one more part of my armour for you", and in saying that, he pulled a shield out from behind his back, as though he had it there the whole time as a surprise.

Surprised Vicki was, but by now had learned to just trust in her Father's goodness.

She looked up at her Father and went to take the shield, as she touched it, the shield became a beautiful plaited leather stock whip, the kind her father used to bring in the cattle at muster time. A little puzzled, but delighted she took the whip, all coiled up like a rope and putting her arm through the centre, put it around her shoulder.

"This is my shield of faith explained Father. It will protect your faith in me from doubt and help you to stand strong in your belief." Said Father

He then reached down and took Vicki by the hand. They started to make their way outside, but before they had taken two steps towards the door, they were outside.

Vicki was so amazed, she was speechless. They continued walking down the driveway and out along the farm laneway towards the horse's paddocks next to Lynda's house.

Chapter Four

The Heart of the Father

Walking along the country lane, with her Father holding her hand, Vicki felt like a happy go lucky young girl again. Even the dark clouds that had blocked out the sunlight for so long, had opened up over Cooinda.

The sun seemed even brighter than ever before. The grass and trees were greener, the flowers more vibrant and alive with colour.

As they got closer to Lynda's place, Vicki noticed they were heading in the direction of the stables, not the house. It was at this point Father stopped and looked down at Vicki, "Stretch out yours hands little one" He said.

Vicki stretched out her hands and to her utter amazement appeared a long horn, the kind from an animal, it was polished and decorated with silver and gold inlay. The beauty of it took her breath away. "What is it Father?" she gasped.

"This is a Yemeni Shofar child. It comes from a large type of antelope called 'the greater Kudu'." Informed Father "this carries the frequencies of My Kingdom and my anointing. When you blow this it will make a sound that resinates with My Kingdom it will be herd in my house, no matter where you are. This is a call to war!" He continued. "My great Army of Hosts will be dispatched immediately." He said with command in His voice. "It will cause utter confusion and calamity among the ranks of the enemy." "Whenever you blow this, my house will hear your call and a door will be opened for you."

"Use the strap to wear it over your back so as even when you ride, it is with you." He instructed.

Vicki took the shofar and put it over her head and her left shoulder as her whip was over her right arm.

They continued on walking in the direction of the Stables. Vicki couldn't help but wonder what her Father will show her next. For the first time in her life she felt like she was loved so much, she was cherished above everything else. She felt she could burst with joy, and eagerly awaited what will come next. Vicki was so happy and light inside she felt like an eight year old girl again with everything good to look forward to in life and she did something she hadn't done since before her dad had died, she started skipping whilst still holding Father's hand. To her utter joy, Father started skipping right alongside her.

They both burst out laughing. They laughed and skipped all the way to the stables.

As they drew closer to the stables, Vicki had tears of joy rolling down her cheeks from laughing so much. She rubbed her eyes, blurry with tears and wondered if she was seeing double.

Looking out over the paddock where the horses were grazing, there should have been two horses, but Vicki was seeing three!

"OH no Father!" she exclaimed, "Someone's horse must have gotten out, look! It's in the paddock with Lynda's horses." "We have to catch it!"

Father lovingly smiled down at Vicki- seeing her heart full of genuine concern for who had lost their horse. As he looked at Vicki, He raised his hand and immediately the mystery horse came straight for them at a steady gallop.

"Woe" cried out Vicki, worried he might not stop in time and hit the fence but Father stepped forward with confidence to greet the horse as he came to an abrupt Holt.

"Vicki my sweet daughter" said Father. "This is Rhema, his name is the spoken word of my spirit, and it means prophecy.

He has come from your words that you spoke into the future, of the horse you would one day own, he is a gift from my own heart to yours and he will fulfil every mission you speak to. He will carry you through every battle and you will be victorious. Together you will ride in 'Victory!'" The Father declared in a loud roaring voice.

Vicki fell to her knees, tears streaming down her cheeks, she tried to speak but she could not get words out. She swallowed hard and managed a croaky voice full of emotion. All she could think to say was "Thank you Father" over and over at His feet.

Her tears fell on His sandals, she noticed scars on his feet, holes that went straight through as though He had been pierced clean through his foot. She knew it was The King she was now with.

Vicki felt The King's hand on her shoulder "Arise Vicki" He said, "come and meet your Horse". Those words rang in Vicki's spirit 'Your Horse' I have my very own horse! Thought Vicki as she got back up to her feet.

"Vicki, this is Rhema" said The King, cordially as if introducing her to Royalty, He bowed forward and directed with his arm sideways like a servant in a house making official introductions.

"He is a special breed of horse that I know will mean a lot to you child, he is a Whaler!" delighted The King.

"These horses mean a lot to me too child. Before your country, Australia was even a nation I fashioned this breed so that they would be sturdy, reliable, steadfast War horses, brave and faithful to their rider with great endurance."

"It was on these horses over 100 years ago, when at that time, your nation was the youngest in the world- when your brave cavalry, The Australian Light horse, rode into a battle that many thousand soldiers had been fighting, but they could not take this ground at Beersheba."

"800 Light horsemen mounted on these whalers charged across the very field where Abraham had stood, the horses did not fail them though starved for water and rest as my spirit was upon them. Your great, great, great grandfather and his men charged through enemy lines and claimed back my land that I had promised to My chosen ones long ago.

On that day my youngest nation of Australia restored my oldest nation of Israel to their promised land on 800 of these divine horses. Fulfilling prophecy. Thus giving rise to the reputation of the 'Sprit of THE ANZACS.'" The King said as He stroked Rhema's face.

"Yes, I know Lord" answered Vicki eagerly, and this hat is part of their uniform still today" she added, as she admired the beauty of Rhema. A beautiful bay, perfect in confirmation and gait. He had the kindest eyes she had seen in a horse and true to the breed, he was solid in colour, no white at all.

"Hi Rhema" Vicki said with such heart felt sincerity as she stretched out her hand to pat her horse for the very first time.

Just as she touched his face, Rhema looked to the side and let out a very loud neigh. This took Vicki by surprise. Out from around the corner of the stables came a beautiful blue cattle dog. He ran straight

up to Rhema, licked Rhema's nose then walked over and sat right beside Vick, as if he had known her all his life.

"Well Hello!" exclaimed Vicki with surprise. "Where did you come from?" she asked as she went to check his collar.

"I can help you there," said The King. "This is Logos." "Hi Logos" Greeted Vicki

"This is your new dog, his name means My Written word. Rhema and Logos are one with each other. They help and support each other. Without Logos, Vicki, you will lose your way and all of your battles so always rely on him together with Rhema and My armour."

"Oh he's beautiful Lord, Thank you. He will go everywhere with me!" Proclaimed Vicki, hugging and patting Logos.

By now Vicki was ecstatically happy, her head was swimming with all she had been gifted by her true Father and The King. She was trying to wrap her head around everything and take it all in.

Swooning with love for her new horse and dog but more than that, for The Father she had longed to know and didn't even realise it. She always felt like there had to be more, as if part of her was missing. There was a void in her heart and in her life. Now she finally knew what was missing and that empty space inside her was gone. In its place was the love of The Father and His Holy Spirit living inside her.

    Saving the Second Kingdom

"This is what I was made for, this is who I am. I am the daughter of The King. I am a warring prophetess!" she thought to herself.

"I am ready to fight in this war!" she shouted out.

"HAHAHA, well you are certainly equipped for it," said The King, "but don't you think you should work with Rhema and Logos for a while. Training and learning to stand in authority. I mean after all you 'ARE' a commander in my army, shouldn't you meet the soldiers you command first?" said the King with a grin as he moved to the right and gestured with his arm, across the front of himself.

Vicky could not grasp what she was seeing, stumbling back against the fence to where Rhema was standing, she didn't dare to take a breath.

In front of her stood huge beings, some of which were gigantic. Some looked so fierce you would have heart failure at the sight, some looked like weapons such as rockets and hammers and some were huge with a square muscular body and hands of fire. They all looked like types of weapons, yet they were beings. Some with beautiful wings of light, some had no wings.

Vicki stood with her mouth gapping open as she glanced sideways at The King for reassurance, her mouth still open as wide as her eyes.

The King turned to Vicki, ignoring the shock on her face and said "This is a part of my Army of Hosts that I have assigned to you and like any army there are rules and regulations. Certain procedures must be followed to make it official.

"To have Hosts assigned to you, you must first invite the Hosts to partner with you" he informed. The King gestured again with his hand and a much decorated scroll appeared suspended in the air in front of Vicki. "My child, simply read out loud what is written on the scroll." With a flick of his finger the scroll, still suspended in the air, unrolled itself for Vicki to read.

Vicki, now regaining her thoughts, walked up to the scroll, cleared her throat and in the loudest voice she could muster after being so freaked out, she read aloud;-

"As an act of my free will I chose to invite The Host Army of Heaven to be my weapon."

"That's it, that's all it takes, well done, Vicki, Welcome to the good fight of faith!" Exclaimed The King happily.

One of the Hosts was kneeling in front of Vicki as she pledged her invitation. He seemed to be in charge of the battalion. He was a bit different to the others. He had the appearance of a man but he was very big and powerful and he had six wings that were silver. They glistened like crystals in the sunlight. Even though he seemed very fierce, he was very majestic. He wore a beautiful red sash across his front and had armour on similar to what Father had given to Vicki.

He was kneeling on one knee with his sword drawn in front of him, the tip sticking in the ground as his hands held the handle and his head bowed down to Vicki.

He rose slowly to his feet and walked to stand directly in front of Vicki. With great reverence he said "It is my great honour to serve The Father with you, your Highness, please allow me to introduce myself. My name is Eli, I am a commander from the tribe of the Royal Guards and these soldiers are my battalion of Hosts." He announced and went on "We are here to fight the enemy alongside you. We will carry out any and all laws and commands that you may decree." Eli informed Vicki.

Vicki was in awe of his reverence to her, he called me 'Your Highness' was swimming around in her thoughts.

"We have much work to do together, but! First," he said with a knowing smile.

"Allow me to complete your armour." Eli raised his hand up and over his shoulder. He plucked out one of his most exquisite silver feathers from his wings, then turned his gaze back to Vicki.

"Your Highness, it is a tradition among the Angelic tribe's to exchange feathers with each other as a sign of everlasting friendship. It is in keeping with this tradition I would have the esteem honour of presenting you with my humble feather, as a sign of our allegiance and everlasting friendship with you. Wear it always to remind you that you have a mighty army at your disposal." As Eli said this he took the feather and placed it in Vicki's slouch hat, right where the emu plume would go. Then he turned and ceremoniously returned to his battalion.

"Thank you Eli, I love it. How perfect." Vicki said as she examined the feather. It was unlike any feather she had ever seen. Instead of being flat it was round like a cylinder and seemed to have a life of its own as it moved independently.

Vicki was so moved by Eli's gesture and all that The Father had done for her, tears once again pooled in her eyes.

The King then stepped up to Vicki and as he put out his hand, a white cloak appeared before him and seemed to just hover there in the air.

It was decorated all over with colourful embroidery. The coloured threads looked to be made of gemstones as they sparkled like diamonds in the sunlight.

The King took hold of the cloak and waved for Vicki to stand in front of Him.

"Vicki, this cloak carries the mantle of a warrior Prophet. This is the anointing over your destiny. It is a weighty mantle but My Holy Spirit will make it light for you to carry."

The King shook the cloak and let it go, it wrapped itself around Vicki. As it did so it turned into a full length driza-bone coat. Which was a traditional long coat made out of canvas that Australian stockmen wore whilst out on muster.

Vicki could feel the weight of her new mantle, but she felt sure she could carry it.

"You are my Warring Prophetess, you will go out to the Nations and be my shining light in the darkness to guide my children." The King prophesied over Vicki. He turned to His Hosts and as they bowed their heads to him, and he was gone.

Looking over the battalion that stood before her, Rhema, Logos and the gifts from The Father. Vicki tried to think of something fitting to say but at first all she could think of in her jumbled thoughts was simply "Thank you, really, thank you so much." She went on "This morning

I woke to a world that was lost, full of hopelessness and despair but now I know all is not lost, there is hope. We, Father's children, we 'are' the answer." She revealed. "I will draw my sword and fight against the enemy and wake up as many of my brothers and sisters along the way as I can. So that they too can join us until the war is over!" Declared Vicki which was met with a resounding "Here - Here!" as the Hosts cheered Vicki.

With a shout from Eli, they all stood at attention and extended their wings (Those that had them). Eli bowed to Vicki and to The Father now standing next to Vicki, he turned to face his elite army and with that they were gone. A gust of wind swept across Vicki's face.

The Father placed his hand on Vicki's shoulder and gently said "come child, Rhema and Logos are waiting to go for their first ride with you and I'm afraid I must be getting back to my Kingdom.

The Father and Vicki both turned back towards Rhema, still standing at the fence waiting patiently with Logos at his feet.

"Father, do you have to go, can't you stay longer?" asked Vicki.

"Vicki my precious child, even though I go to my Kingdom know in your heart that I am always with you, as I have been from the start. I just needed you to seek me, allowing me to reveal myself to you."

"Now that you have awaken from your slumber, you will always hear my still, small voice if you listen, just as I hear yours." He said.

"Logos will help guide you and Rhema will carry you through every battle faithfully. He will never fail you. Now come and hop on your horse" He added. Knowing how happy it would make Vicki to finally ride her very own horse and it will buffer her feelings once He has left.

Vicki was very excited about her horse and eagerly walked away from The Father towards the tack room in the stables.

"Vicki child, where are you going? Asked The Father, knowing full well what Vicki was thinking.

"I am just going to grab a saddle and bridle to saddle him up" She answered.

A huge smile grew across Fathers face, it seemed to light up the already bright day. One of The Fathers favourite things to do is to surprise his children and lavish them with gifts. He loves to be extravagant with his children.

"Vicki, there's no need, look!" He said, pointing at Rhema, smiling away. Knowing he was fulfilling his daughters heart's desire.

There Rhema stood completely saddled up and ready to go. "You didn't think I'd give you half a gift, did you, HAHAHA." He laughed with delight.

Vicki ran to her Father with tears of joy in her eyes and a heart full of love and belonging. Father spoke to Rhema "come" he said, and in that instant Rhema was on the outside of the fence, head down nuzzling Vicki.

Vicki laughed with delight. Is there anything my Father cannot do, she thought to herself.

"No nothing!" answered The Father with a laugh.

Vicki burst out laughing she and The Father laughed and laughed until tears rolled down their faces and Vicki's tummy hurt.

Father gathered Rhema's reigns and held them. "Jump up" He said and as he spoke Vicki found herself up on Rhema's back. The saddle fit perfectly even the stirrups were the right length. She placed her feet in the stirrups and knew it was time for her Father to return to His Kingdom. She had mixed feelings of sadness and elated joy.

The Father still holding the reigns, looked up at Vicki and asked "Now how does that feel?" Vicki's reply filled The Fathers heart with joy. "Like we were meant for each other Father." She said with the biggest smile.

"Now I know that most whalers are solid colour with not a lot of white markings but before I go I just want to do this one thing" He said with a grin and he took his pointer finger and drew on Rhema's forehead in a zig zag kind of pattern.

"There!" He said, grinning ear to ear. "Now you are all set."

Vicki was so curious to see what Father meant that she jumped down and went to the front of Rhema, where Father stood. She looked puzzled at the white marking Rhema now had on his forehead, it looked like a lightning bolt.

Then she remembered what Paul had said about The Father's sense of humour and how both he and Ethan had lightning bolts on their gifts.

Father chuckled and said "Every time the enemy looks upon Rhema's face, he will be reminded of the very beginning when he first started this war in My Kingdom. The Hosts defeated him and his army and I threw him out with a bolt of lightning that stripped him of all his power I had anointed him with. "They both laughed at the thought.

The Father then hugged Vicki and said "Go on, jump up!" gesturing to Rhema.

Vicki climbed up and got settled. Father, standing by her side solemnly said "Remember my child, you are My Precious daughter, and I am with you always everywhere you go. We will speak every day, you will see me again."

"But how Father? How shall I hear you speak to me?" Vicki asked.

"Whenever you want to speak to me just go to a place, somewhere that you can quiet your thoughts and speak to me, just as you are now. If you listen, you will hear my still, small voice inside you. I always answer my children, though sometimes it's not the answer you wanted or expected."

"Remember Child, I have many children, you are not alone Vicki, go and find your brothers and sisters who are already awake in me and help to unit them. Wake as many others out of their slumber as you can. United you will be my remnant, my ecclesia. I left My Word on your bed, study it child, it is a guide to help all my children navigate through life in this broken Kingdom."

With that, Father turned and started walking back towards the laneway. Vicki turned back to wave one last time and He was gone.

Chapter Five
It Is Time

The next few months were busy for Vicki, she spent all her time reading Her Father's book, His word was like food for her soul. It grounded her and helped her to grow in the authority The King had anointed her with.

She spent hour's everyday riding Rhema with Logos faithfully following alongside.

Vicki had become very efficient in using the gifts of her armour and all her weapons.

She had managed to keep the evil army from inflicting more darkness on Cooinda. The sky was a deep blue and the sun shone diligently over it. Their crops and pastures flourished but when she looked beyond Cooinda's boundaries, all she could see were dark skies to the horizon.

Vicki sat upon Rhema, looking out over the vast land before her. She remembered the carefree adventures she had, riding Gisselle across the country side and stopping at her favourite place, the creek flats. Watching all the native animals meander along the creek banks as they drank. Not even seeming to mind Vicki's presence only a short distance away.

As she sat, reminiscing, Vicki realised how much she had missed riding to the creek. It had been almost a year now since the evil king and his army convinced all the nations of the great lie and locked down the world. Not to venture out lest they fall under a curse and die. The people were already under a spell that put their minds to sleep. So they blindly followed the wicked decree and in doing so, gave all their authority over to the evil king and his wicked army. Thus allowing them to wreak all sorts of strife and heartache upon the people and their lands.

"This is why I need my children, my ecclesia to fight" Vicki heard her Father say to her in her spirit." "It is time." She heard. It was in that moment Vicki knew it was time for her to join in fighting the war and boldly go where the Lord would lead her. Mending the people and the land as she went.

Vicki went home to pack some supervisions not knowing how long she would be gone. She left a note for her mother and loaded Rhema up with supplies.

She put on her armour and blew her shofar "Come on Rhema, let's go, come Logos" she called and rode out.

Riding the trail through the valley's Vicki was very sad to see all the damage and destruction the darkness had caused to the surrounding farms.

Where once there were lush pastures with fat cattle and sheep dotted all over, were now desolate and abandoned of livestock. Tumbleweed blowing across the baron fields.

Vicki swallowed her sorrow at this sight, she knew this meant the families that had lived here for generations had now been force to leave the only homes they had known and all their family history.

Her thoughts went to the creek flats "Come on Rhema let's get to the creek flats" she said as she pushed him into a canter.

The once beautiful crystal clear spring fed creek was green and murky with a toxic looking film covering the surface. The fertile green oasis was now a toxic wasteland.

The evil army had been mining for lithium to make batteries for electric cars of all things, directly upstream from this area and had poisoned the water. It was seeping into the soil effecting the surrounding fauna and flora.

This broke Vicki's heart, Rhema and Logos held their heads low, Vicki's spirit began to rise up in her, she blew her shofar over the land and drew her sword decreeing victory and speaking healing over the devastated land. She decreed "I crush all of the enemies' strongholds, shred every platform built over this area now. I bind the powers and principalities working here and I command the Hosts to take them away in chains now. I cast their power to the sea and command purification, fertility and life abundant over this land in The Name of The King."

Then turning to the direction of where the enemy were mining, pointing her sword to them she decreed that their equipment will fail. They will no longer detect nor find any lithium to mine and their own darkness shall rain down on them and strike the ground with lightning until they leave the area. As it is in my Father's Kingdom, so shall it be here" she decreed

Vicki asked her Father to anoint her words as she called for Eli.

In an instant Eli was standing before her he bowed his head but said nothing "Eli send 100 Hosts to take up these swords and go carry out my decree over this land." Vicki commanded and then said "Eli you and the rest of the battalion stay with me as I continue to mount Yarramundi,

Father is leading me there. We will fight our way to the top to destroy the enemy's stronghold upon this mountain!"

"Yes, by taking back Mt Yarramundi, we are effectively cutting out the enemy's tongue. It is from there they are controlling what the people are being told. Thus they control the fake narrative being spoken over the people" Agreed Eli.

"In the name of The King let's go!" Cried Vicki as she galloped off. Eli and the remaining Hosts surrounded Vicki as they swiftly made their way to mount Yarramundi.

Along bush tracks and through valley's they went. Until they came to the foothills of mount Yarramundi. They came to a clearing where Vicki stopped and looked up at the huge Mountain. It leered over the hills, encumbering the sky above in its vastness.

"That is a lot of territory to take Eli" admitted Vicki, she went on "I believe we can take this mountain back or Father would not have sent us here!" she said as her faith rose up inside her.

Right then she heard a familiar voice ring out through the surrounding bush, "G'day Tidda, long time no see."

Vicki's eyes grew as wide as her smile, there was only one person that ever called her Tidda (meaning sister or friend in some aboriginal languages) "Yarran!" called Vicki. She had not seen her friend in months due to the lockdowns. Her eyes scoured the tree line to see where he was "Yarran, where are you?" she called out with excitement.

"Right here" he said laughing right behind her. "Oh gosh" laughed Vicki, "trapping brumbies has made you stealth" she said.

"Nice horse Vicki and since when do you have a dog?"

"Oh Yarran I have so much to tell you... Like I met The Father!!!" She exclaimed.

"He gave me all these gifts and my horse Rhema and well, you seem to have already made friends with Logos" she chuckled as Yarran was patting Logos on his head.

"Oh that is awesome Vicki, you look so happy. I'm really glad and I love Rhema, he's a beauty" said Yarran as he patted Rhema's face not noticing the tell tail marking on his forehead.

                                    Saving the Second Kingdom

"Well" said Yarran, "I've got some news for you too" he announced. He turned his head and let out a very loud whistle. There was a rustling in the bushes for a moment and out came a beautiful black horse closely followed by a dingo that was as red as the outback.

"Vicki, this is Prophet, he is a brumby from the Victorian snowy high country and this character is Preacher, a pure Alpine dingo, now sadly one of the most endangered of all dingos" Yarran explained. "Wow Yarran, I love Prophet he really is nice, I love the crimp in his mane and tail, gorgeous and Preacher is just the best, what a beautiful colour" she said

Vicki couldn't help but notice a distinct white mark on Prophet's forehead shaped suspiciously like a bolt of lightning and the white patch on Preachers chest, indicative of the alpine dingo, also was a lightning bolt. This made Vicki laugh with glee as she saw her Father's imprint on both Prophet and Preacher and she knew in that moment Yarran had been sent to meet up with her.

"Yarran, look at Rhema's forehead" she said waiting for his reaction. Yarran went back over and lifted up Rhema's lush thick forelock to reveal the rest of his white marking hidden under it, and he let out a resounding "YES"

"Vicki", he said "I was sent here by The Father as his prophet to find his warring Prophetess and help her in the battle to take back this mountain, I cannot believe it's you Vicki, that's awesome" he explained. Yarran was in awe of the Fathers plan and how he loves to surprise his children.

He continued" When I saw you Vicki, I was coming to tell you to go home until it was safe here once again." They both laughed "Oh this is awesome Father, thank you "Squealed Vicki in sheer delight.

Yarran jumped up on Prophet and they rode into the hills with mount Yarramundi looming overhead. All the while chatting and sharing their experiences with the king and their army of Hosts until they had reached the mountain.

Chapter Six
Humble Heroes

Standing at the base of mount Yarramundi, Vicki and Yarran gazed up at the ominous mountain looming overhead. They looked at each other, both thinking the same thing... "We need to speak with Father" Yarran said breaking the silence "We need to ask him for

a strategy before we start up the trail, let's camp here for the night" He added." Yes definitely!" Vicki agreed.

She went on "When Father gave me this assignment He showed me that the enemy have taken over this entire mountain all the way to the top. As it is from this mountain that all communication is sent out to the people. By controlling from the very top, they control everything the people are told through all media outlets. So they dictate everything the people hear and everything they do not want the people to hear they deem as lies. The people have no reason to suspect they are being deceived. They do not see nor understand that by going along in agreement with the wicked agendas of the evil king, they are giving over their authority and in doing so handing him their power to accomplish his wicked plots and schemes. The evil king used witches to put spells over the people effectively blindfolding them to the truth. So we can expect him and his evil band of clowns to put up a fight. They will plot against us and devise all manner of deception to try to stop us because he will lose a huge part of his control over the nations when we take this mountain back." She explained.

"We need to remember our King already won the great battle long ago, so the evil king and all his cohorts are already defeated. We just have to let them know that we know that too. In fact, Father said that he is so beneath us, he is under our feet and that is exactly where I intend to keep him." Yarran added.

Vicki Decreed Victory over mount Yarramundi as she grabbed for her shofar, Yarran did so as well and they both began to sound a call to war.

Within seconds they were surrounded by Eli and the Hosts awaiting their new orders, while Vicki and Yarran were both speaking with the King. He told them he had left instructions in his book of truth- that his children were to rule and reign from each mountain top as they take them back from the evil one- Never to allow their authority to be taken away from the seven great mountains of rule again. Until the day He will return to live among us and take His rightful place as the King. Vicki and Yarran took this very seriously.

The next morning they packed up camp and saddled the horses. As they mounted up, they drew their swords and began to decree that the powers and principalities and the rulers in high places, ruling at the very top were there illegally as a defeated foe and as so, to be bound in chains. Eli take these decrees and capture the rulers in high places, when they are in chains take them to the courts of the Father's Kingdom for judgement. Leave half the battalion here to help us clear out the rest of the mountain while you battle the high places.

In a flash Eli and half the Hosts were gone. Yarran and Vicki started the long trek up the side of the steep mountain. They could hear the clanking of swords and saw flashes of light coming from the huge dark clouds that covered the top of the mountain. At one point the fierce battle lit up the dark sky like a lightning storm. The battle seemed to get higher and higher in the sky, they could see the flashes of the Hosts' swords as they battled against the principality and his high ranking soldiers. It was quite a sight to see these huge host angels fighting against the soldiers of darkness.

Then both Vicki and Yarran heard the King say "send them more swords, they need more weapons, keep speaking decrees over the battle"

Vicki and Yarran riding as fast as they could along the rough mountain trail sounded their shofars again, knowing it would send confusion throughout the ranks of the enemy. Then Yarran remembered something he had read in Fathers book, "It is written that whatever I bind on earth is bound from the Kingdom and whatever I loose on earth shall be loosed from the Kingdom. I decree we bind the rulers of darkness over this mountain and every agent in this army of darkness. We bind your power and cut all communication within your ranks in the name of the King." He decreed, continuing he shouted "We loose VICTORY over this mountain and this battle I decree now by the power of our King -victory" Eli came charging out of the cloud, with his magnificent wings outstretched he swooped down and took up Yarrans decrees that were hovering above him "good job young prophets, don't stop, keep decreeing victory" encouraged Eli as he grabbed the weapons and whoosh, he was off back into the battle.

Vicki blew her shofar again as they continued forging ahead. Preparing for further battles they both took their shields in hand ready to face the enemy at any given time.

Right then there was a flash of light and a loud clap of thunder that sounded like a thousand lions roaring. Vicki and Yarran came to an abrupt holt and as the two prophets looked on, they noticed Eli was wounded and some of the other Hosts were looking injured and weary.

Vicki turned to the Hosts that had remained on the ground with them and asked "Hosts, will Eli be ok? He is wounded and some of the Hosts are too. Will they be able to keep fighting? "

One of the Hosts came to the front, he was a strange looking creature. He was very tall with arms and legs of solid muscle, his legs were as thick as tree trunks. He had a thick muscly neck with a round head and his body seemed to wobble as if he was made of liquid. His wings were of light and his hair was of fire. His penetrating eyes were the colour of amber and glowed like flames. He introduced himself to the prophets.

"Hi, my name is Athos but everyone calls me Jellyroll, Jelly for short." He said smiling, knowing this would amuse Vicki and Yarran.

"Ha-ha-ha 'Jellyroll', I love that," laughed Vicki." Jelly can we help Eli and the Hosts?" She asked concerned for them.

Jelly was touched by their concern for the Hosts and said. "If Eli and the Hosts look battle worn then you can be assured the enemy look worse" and with a chuckle he continued "Your decrees empowered them but you still need to keep believing in faith and decreeing out loud until we have victory. Your spoken decrees are like extra battery charge to renew their strength, it will give the Angels what they need to remain victorious. As for their injuries, The King, our commander and chief will heal them all, they will be ok, do not worry" Jelly explained.

"Thank you Jelly that makes me feel better!" said Vicki.

Yarran was dying to know why they call him Jellyroll. He didn't want to be rude but curiosity got the better of him and he just had to ask

"Um, if you don't mind" He said sheepishly "Can I ask why they call you Jellyroll?" All the Hosts standing before them laughed quietly to themselves, they loved Yarran's curious spirit. Vicki gave Yarran a look as if he was being rude, but secretly she was so glad he asked as she was dying to know as well.

Jelly laughed with delight as he loved mankind but had never gotten to actually speak with any before now and he was elated that Yarran had asked. "I thought you would never ask" He said gleefully. "Here I'll show you" and with that he flew up into the sky. His body grew very large, it engulfed his head, arms, legs even his wings until he was a huge long round roll. He seemed to vibrate which made his entire body wobble like jelly. The vibration made a sound like rolling thunder. He started rolling and vibrating faster and faster until he was like a tornado but on its side and with a whirring gush of wind. Up he went gaining speed and momentum as he rose higher and higher up into the sky until he disappeared into the black cloud above where Eli and the Hosts were battling the enemy.

"We declare victory over this mountain" shouted both Vicki and Yarran. They were both wondering what Jelly would do next.

There were sounds of rolling thunder coming from the clouds and then strange noises that sounded like pins in a bowling alley being knocked down. The remaining Hosts were laughing as they knew what this sound meant.

Two hideously ugly dark creatures, their wings in tatters came bounding out of the cloud they seemed to be trying to escape something, it was like a scene from a cartoon, their ugly faces looking behind them. There was a clap of thunder rolling, it got louder and louder. The two ugly beasts let out a blood curdling shriek. A sound as hideous as they were. Then suddenly it was clear why. Jelly came bursting out of the cloud, rolling like thunder. The noise he made weakened the two fleeing beasts. As he rolled right over the top of them, they seemed to get swallowed up in Jelly's tornado. The shrieks of horror continued until they were spat out of his whirling mass.

They were flung out with such force, they flew backwards for miles. A portal opened up in the sky and another Angel emerged. He was huge, taller than a big city sky scraper, his foot was as big as a house. He was all golden and shone brighter than the sun and in his hands he had chains, huge chains that looked to be made of lightening. They flashed like electricity sparking. The mighty angel had hold of the end of the chains that were attached to leg irons, he gave a powerful flick to the chains in a whip cracking motion and sent the leg irons out to meet the two dark creatures. They were well aware of the chains coming for them. They were trying to scramble out of reach but were unable to escape, still trapped in the momentum of being thrust out by Jelly. Vicki and Yarran watched these events unfold wide eyed and white knuckled. Popcorn would have been great at this moment.

'Snap' the chains caught them and snapped shut loudly around their legs, then continued to spin around them until they were wrapped in a cocoon of chains. The huge angel gathered up the slack of the chains, slung it over his shoulder and began to drag the dark creatures, still struggling and screeching back through the portal, to the courts of the Fathers Kingdom for judgement.

A chorus of cheers rang out from the two young prophets amazed by what they had just witnessed, the Hosts were dancing and singing praise to The King, Vicki and Yarran joined in. Their voices turned into sweet smelling smoke like incense and was carried all the way up past the cloud where the battle still raged right up through the portal as it disappeared.

Jellyroll reformed back into his normal self and started descending down to the cheers and singing. He was grinning from ear to ear and could barely contain himself. "Woo-hoo" he yelled down to the rest of his battalion waiting for him. "That was fun!" he yelled. His laughter filled the air as he made his decent.

"That was the coolest thing we've ever seen "Vicki and Yarran both agreed and were very excited. "Wow Jelly now we get why they call you Jellyroll" said Yarran.

"Absolutely, you are awesome!" cried Vicki.

But when Jelly heard this he humbled himself, "No, No not me, don't admire me, I am just a servant of the King, please do not praise me, I was just having fun doing what I was created to do. It is the King that deserves ALL praise and Glory".

This humbled Vicki "Yes Jelly, you are so right. It is easy to get caught up in moments when we accomplish something and become filled with pride. We forget we can do nothing without Father, He should always receive the thanks and praise not us. Thank you for reminding us." She said thoughtfully.

"Young prophets you will accomplish much for the Kingdom. You are the Father's delight, fear not." Jelly said which was followed by a loud "Here- here" from the Hosts in agreement.

"Now let's go take this mountain back, come on, I saw an enemy stronghold not far from here while I was up high." Declared Jelly "sound the shofars" he called with excitement and expectation.

They all charged ahead, the two prophets on their mounts surrounded by the remaining battalion of angelic Hosts. Vicki was thinking about what Jelly had said, how he thoroughly enjoyed himself just doing what he was made to do. How he just came alive in those moments. She related it back to herself and figured Yarran was the same judging by his face. She had never felt so alive and so fulfilled than now actively being about her Fathers business.

This is what I was created to do, she thought to herself. This is my destiny "Woo-Hoo" she blurted out and blew her shofar at the gallop. Rhema neighed, nostrils flared, catching Vicki's excitement. On they pushed Preparing to take out that enemy stronghold Jelly had spotted up ahead.

Chapter Seven
The Winds of Change

The shofars could be heard right up the mountain as the prophets forged ahead. With every echo of the shofars the enemy shuddered unable to operate.

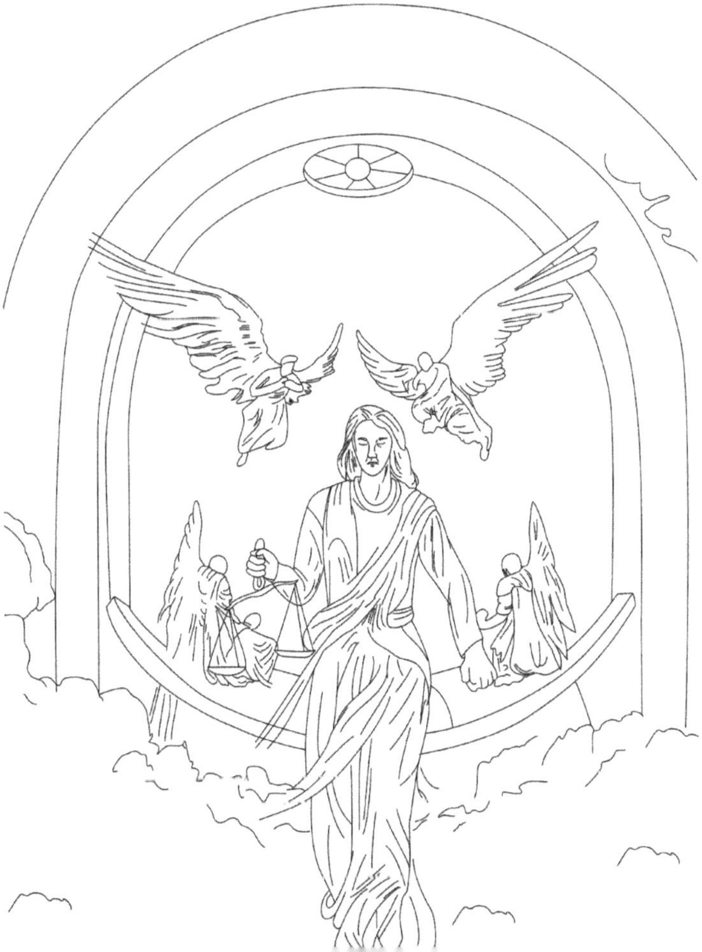

Vicki could feel the air growing heavy, she sensed the stronghold was near. Jelly announced "We are here" and everyone slowed to a walking pace. Yarran started taking authority and claiming victory over the enemy stronghold reminding them they are already defeated, they have no legal right to be there. He evicted them in the name of the King. Vicki all the while in agreement with him. They blew their shofars and commanded the Hosts to shred any platforms they may have built and crush the stronghold. Taking every prisoner to the Fathers courts to be judged for their crimes.

As soon as the Hosts were released cheers of very loud enthusiastic Woo-Hoo's rang out through a rush of wind as the Hosts gathered up all the swords of decrees and flew eagerly to battle. Vicki and Yarran watching on, continuously declaring victory over the enemy and blowing their shofars.

This time the battle was not high in the clouds, but right there in front of them where the stronghold was because, darkness must be fought in the territory that it holds. The enemy commanders are called the rulers of darkness, they are powers and principalities. They are fought up high in the clouds where they reign from because they rule and reign in high places. So they must be unseated from where their thrown is. Once they are removed in the spirit realm, only then what is being influenced by them in the natural world can be undone. So by first taking away the authority they have in the spiritual world, you can then take back the authority in the natural world and things will be set right again on mount Yarramundi.

That is why this battle was not up high but right there where the enemy were sending out lies and deception to the people. All the radio stations and newspapers as well as all TV stations and social Medias were here on this mountain under the influence of this wicked stronghold.

All the people who worked there were either wicked themselves, being bribed, blackmailed or just very fearful and unable to do anything. Either way most are corrupt and have to be removed from their positions so that the righteous ecclesia can take their places and start waking the people up out of this spell they are under by speaking the truth.

With that in mind Vicki and Yarran kept speaking out their decrees. Vicki decreed "I bind now all enemy agents influencing and operating through these Medias and I evict them from this mountain. I cut all communication among their ranks and I bind them in chains to be taken to Judgement In the name of The King."

When her words rang out into the atmosphere there was a shift that could be felt. The air was no longer heavy and they watched as her words turned into hundreds of swords for the Hosts to use against the enemy. It was amazing to watch.

The Hosts battled intensely, certain of their victory. The enemy failing, they could not withstand the sheer force of the Hosts. They looked like filthy vermin who were trying to escape a sinking ship, scurrying from their imminent doom. They were disgusting fowl creatures to look at. Most were horribly disfigured and tattered like old rags. Vicki and Yarran were loathed to look upon them but grateful Father was allowing them the gift of spiritual sight, so they can watch.

Suddenly there was a rumbling in the earth followed by a sound like rolling thunder. Jelly was doing his roll. "Ha-ha-ha go Jelly" rang out as the two prophets cheered with joy.

A portal opened up a little way from where Vicki and Yarran were, and out stepped a beautiful Angel. He was glowing like the sun and was carrying with him a set of scales. "This is my Angel of justice" They heard the Father say in a booming voice "He and my angels of change will bring my law and order back to this mountain. The wicked will be dealt with and all those who did their bidding and refuse to repent will be removed, never to be heard of again." Declared Father.

Then legions upon legions of angels stepped through the open portal. Too many to even try to guess a number. The last angel that stepped through was the angel with chains. Jelly was spitting out the vile creatures with even more force the previous time. They flew helpless, legs and arms flailing about. A horrible blood curdling screech coming from them as the large angel gathered his chains and flicked them like whips. They caught their prey and wrapped around them until the beasts were cocooned in chains. He then dragged them off like a big sack of potatoes back through the portal for judgement.

The portal closed and it was all over. Peace fell upon the battle ground. The prophets sounded their shofars with triumph. They had crushed the stronghold and the enemy were in chains taken to judgement.

"No time to celebrate yet" Vicki announced, "We still need to crush two more strongholds. The next one is more powerful than this one was, it is the television networks. Only after that can we take the biggest one of all" She added.

"Yes let's go" cried Yarran and once again they were off. The two prophets at the gallop surrounded by half a battalion of Hosts. It was a sight to see.

The Lord Sabaoth spoke to the prophets and explained to them that by sending the Hosts ahead, it would make the track easier for them to travel along as it was getting rough, full of obstacles and traps set by the enemy to overcome them. "The Hosts will smooth the way for you" Said Lord Sabaoth.

Vicki and Yarran pulled up the horses and called Jellyroll. "Jelly, the Lord has told us to send you all ahead to smooth the way and remove the obstacles and engage the enemy in his camp, Go!" Commanded Vicki.

"We will follow along but our decrees will go before you." Yarran added and he immediately started decrees of victory and binding the enemy in chains. Both prophets blew their shofars and drew their shields ready to deflect anything the enemy may throw at them.

The air became increasingly thick again and straight away they both knew they were getting close. 'Ssshhew' something whizzed right by Vicki's face 'Ssshhew' and another just missed Yarran.

"They are shooting fiery darts at us" said Yarran. Then a whole slew of darts came at them. They hit their shields and fell to the ground.

"They are trying to get us off track. This is a sign we are a threat to them" informed Vicki.

"Yeah for sure" agreed Yarran "and I'm about to become an even bigger threat" Yarran pulled his shield up in front of him and commanded every dart to become a boomerang and turn right back to the enemy" He thanked the Father for his protection then laughed "I never could get the hang of throwing those- things, my dad tried and tried to teach me, who knew, all I had to do was speak it" they both laughed at the irony and carried on. Unwilling to allow the enemy's attempts of distraction to lead them off track.

They didn't get too much further along before the ground started shaking and a familiar rumble could be heard. The prophets looked at each other and at the same time said "Jellyroll" Laughing as they reached for their shofars and sounded a victory call. They could hear the shrieks of the terrified enemy as Jelly engaged them. They hurried along the path to get to the battle scene. Vicki and Yarran arrived just in time to see the angel with chains dragging his prisoners off to judgement. Vicki stood up in her stirrups and spoke to the Hosts.

"We have one more stronghold to crush, this one will have high platforms that the enemy keep watch from. It allows them to see what is coming much further away because they lookout from the top. These platforms will need to be shredded so that the stronghold can be crushed, let's go take this mountain back" she cried and they were off again.

Their attention turned back to Eli and his Hosts, still battling in the high places as flashes of light throughout the dark cloud lit it up like morning. Then thunderous roars started echoing through the air bellowing out into the atmosphere. The prophets both again decreed victory in high places, they bound the powers and principalities and evicted them from their thrown in chains never to return nor send replacements. Eli like a flash of light swooped down to take the decrees and use them.

Chapter Eight
Discernment

The track to the top of the mountain was steep and full of obstacles, it was to be a challenging path for Vicki and Yarran to conquer. With Lord Sabaoth to guide them they felt strong in their conviction to reach the top. They came to a small clearing

at the side of the path. They hopped down from the horses and let them graze freely. "We should camp here tonight" Vicki suggested not realising how tired she was till they had stopped. Yarran agreed.

The Hosts surrounded the two prophets as they got down on their knees and began to speak to the King. They asked the King for a war strategy to use against the enemy at the next stronghold. They waited patiently for his answer. Some time passed, the two prophets were still on their knees thanking their Father for everything he has done for them and for the victory they were about to receive. As they knew their victory had already been foretold by prophets long ago.

A beautiful angel appeared in front of them and said "Young prophets, I have been sent by Yahweh the Commander of The Host Army. I am to tell you about your next mission" he said in a gentle yet commanding voice. He continued "this next stronghold is the biggest one, and the most corrupt because it has become the most used of all the Medias. More so by design because of the lockdowns. The people turned to this media as a main form of communication and socialising as they are not permitted to go out and meet up with loved ones freely. Out of sheer loneliness in some cases, it has become the most widely used form of communication. Not just here in Australia but the entire world is entrenched in its web of lies and deceit." He continued.

"It has become a powerful tool for those few people at the very top, the elites, to use to deploy their wicked plots and schemes shown to them by the evil king named Baal that they worship. Knowing it has the widest audience. They are the most corrupt wicked people, they bow down to Baal and commit many atrocities against mankind even against children. Nothing is out of bounds to them as they are without conscience" The angel paused, he took a small vial from his golden belt and said, "I am to anoint you with fresh oil" Vicki and Yarran both still kneeling bowed their heads as the angel approached them with the vial. He gently poured the oil over the prophet's heads and then said "Arise true and faithful servants of the King. This fresh anointing will give you the strength you will need to endure and overcome all the enemy's plots against you as you continue on your path". With that the angel was gone.

The next morning both Vicki and Yarran felt stronger than ever before both spiritually and naturally. They mounted their horses and blew their shofars together knowing the frequency of the sound would help Eli and the Hosts as they continued their long battle. Evident by the constant clashing visible as light in the darkness of the clouds.

Their attention turned back to the task ahead of them. "Ok Jelly" Called Vicki "Go on ahead of us and smooth the way so that we can travel faster. Take the Hosts and engage all the enemy along the way. Send them to Father in chains" she added. And in a gush of wind they were off. Yarran all the while had been sending out decrees of eviction for the enemy and victory for the Hosts. Ensuring they had many weapons in their arsenals to help them.

They had been travelling along for a short while and aside from noticing an eerie silence with the absence of birds and wildlife they were making good time ascending the mountain track. Yarran and Vicki were both admiring all the native plant life and the occasional view of the valley below through breaks in the tall trees as by now they were quite high up.

Suddenly the silence was broken by the sound of Preacher and Logos barking intently at something. They were out scouting up ahead as usual but this was not normal for them. Vicki whistled to call them back. They came running back as fast as they could thrashing about through the thick bush. Panting heavily and acting very excited and out of character.

"We better go check out what they found Vicki" said Yarran. "Preacher seek!" He ordered. Both dogs went tearing off, Vicki and Yarran had to ride hard to keep them in sight. The dogs went around a bend and the prophets lost sight of them.

"I think if we just keep following this track we will find them" Vicki suggested.

"Yeah try to keep an ear out for them I recon we will hear them" added Yarran. So they kept going at a swift pace, along the winding track that their dogs had led them to.

They could hear a 'yip' every now and then which gave them a clue as to where the dogs were. Then the barking started again. As the prophets drew closer they could hear a female voice trying to shew the dogs away. Vicki and Yarran looked at each other with surprise "maybe someone is hurt or lost" shrugged Yarran.

"Guess we are about to find out" answered Vicki.

They had them in sight, the dogs both barking at the bushes in front of them. A woman's voice was cussing at the dogs and an arm appeared out of the bushes motioning for the dogs to leave. The prophets came up on the scene with thundering hoof beats. They both jumped down before the horses had even stopped. Reins in hand they approached the woman cautiously as they didn't want to add more calamity to the scene.

"Logos, Preacher, Here" Vicki called the dogs back, they did come but the dogs stayed in front as if protecting Vicki and Yarran as they both walked calmly towards the bush where the woman was hiding.

"Excuse me, Hi" said Vicki "We are sorry if our dogs scared you".

A very angry voice came back at Vicki full of cursing "These BLEEPING dogs should be BLEEPING muzzled and shot. They shouldn't be running free terrorising innocent people" The woman hissed at them.

As the prophets looked down into the bush they saw a small middle aged woman, dressed in black clothes more suited to an office worker. She had long dark brown hair and a very sour wrinkled face. She seemed even more bothered by the arrival of the prophets.

At first glance both Vicki and Yarran put the woman's bad behaviour down to fear. She seemed scared of Logos and Preacher and of Rhema and Prophet. A lot of people are scared of horses as they find their size intimidating or they had a bad experience, so that was fairly normal they thought to themselves with their forgiving natures. The prophets ignored the woman's bad language and apologised again for their dogs' behaviour. They walked back a few steps and told the dogs to stay and asked if they could help the lady out of the bush, thinking she must have fallen in when the dogs came up on her.

"No-no! I'm fine" she answered "just keep those mutts away" she added with a scrawl. Then she scrambled back up onto the track revealing a narrow somewhat hidden track behind her. It was on seeing this track the prophets realised that she must have come from there and not fallen in the bush as they first thought.

When she got herself up, she fixed her clothes and brushed herself down. "So who do I have here and what are you two doing this far up the side of the mountain?" The woman asked. "My name is Yarran and this is my friend Vicki, we are prophets sent by our Father to carry out a mission" explained Yarran.

"What is your name? And how did you come to be out here on a mountain all alone with no supplies or proper clothes? Are you lost? Do you need help?" Vicki asked out of concern for the woman.

"Whoa, so many questions" was the woman's response. "Prophets on a mission you say." Her face turned from an angry scrawl to a friendly smile "My name is Claire" she added.

"Claire, how did you come to be all the way out here?" asked Vicki again.

Claire seemed flustered for a second and then answered "Well you see I was working for the social media network Metface when a workmate of mine did some really bad things and blamed them on me. Then to silence me, she forced me in her car, drove as close as she could to this track, then we walked to get here. She threw me down that little track I just came from and she left me there hoping I would get lost and perish before anyone found me. But look you found me. I'm saved!" Claire cheered but it sounded more like mocking.

Vicki's spirit was uneasy and she was observing the way the dogs were staying in-between Claire and herself. Yarran was still looking down the path where Claire had been. He noticed the track was well worn which was odd considering how secluded it was. Looking further into the bushes he could see a small clearing and he heard Lord Sabaoth say "Claire is a witch, that is where her coven's alter to Baal

Saving the Second Kingdom

is". He turned his head in time to see Claire reaching her hand out to offer Prophet something to eat. Yarran couldn't see what it was and Vicki's attention was on the dogs but he knew with every fibre of his being in that moment, Claire was a witch and she was going to poison Prophet.

He quickly lunged forward and knocked Claire's hand away from the horse's mouth. A small gel vial feel out of Claire's hand and rolled along the ground away from them. Vicki wondered what Yarran was doing as they all scrambled to pick up the vial.

"Leave it, it's mine" insisted Claire.

Yarran quickly snatched it up in his hand. Ignoring Claire's protest. He held it up to his nose "what is this?" He demanded glaring at Claire.

"It's just some treats I make for the horses that live in this National Park. It's good for them, I promise" answered Claire.

Yarran smelt it "what is it?" asked Vicki.

"Smells like apple" said Yarran as he went to break it open to smell the liquid inside.

"See, I told you. It's just concentrated apple juice" Claire added not knowing that Yarran's family were excellent trackers and Yarran had become very good at identifying substances used for poison. He had unfortunately had plenty of practise honing his skills over the last few years with his dad. He held up the open vial to smell the liquid inside.

"Oh, no need for all that, just throw it in the bushes" insisted Claire.

"I'll be the judge of that" answered Yarran as the contents of the vial spilled out onto the palm of his hand.

"It's funny apple juice" he said mocking Claire. "No odour at all", he took the tiniest sample onto his finger tip and just barely tipped his tongue into it. He spat out the bitter tasting liquid instantly.

"It is oleander" he declared. "She was going to poison Prophet Vicki" he announced in disbelief. Vicki instantly stepped back from Claire and released the dogs to stand guard and not let her move.

"Why would you do such a cruel ghastly thing?" asked Vicki, horrified at the thought someone could have such a cold hard heart. Claire stood chuckling to herself under her breath. Not seeming to care at all only, for the fact she was stopped.

"Vicki, I heard Lord Sabaoth say that she is a witch that worships Baal and that path Claire was on leads to an alter they have been using. I'm pretty sure they are the ones that have been poisoning the brumby's because I've seen this vial of oleander extract before. In the water holes the brumby's frequent not to mention all the other wildlife. Sometimes the broken vials would still be floating on top of the water not quite dissolved or dropped just on the edge of the water." Informed Yarran.

Vicki was so heartbroken at the cruelty, her thoughts went out to all the animals that had suffered but she turned to Claire and said "I forgive you and I will ask my Father to forgive you for these atrocities against his beautiful creations. I will ask he delivers you from this bondage of baal worship. My King can break off the chains of bondage and you can know spiritual freedom if you will repent and surrender your heart to Him" Vicki said with her heart in her throat and tears streaming down her cheeks still thinking of all the poor innocent animals that suffered from Claire's poison. Claire hissed at Vicki's words like a snake. She started cursing at the two prophets again.

Yarran and Vicki both knew Claire was full of bad spirits that had been able to enter her life because of her worship of the evil one and they knew that is was those bad spirits now speaking through Claire. They also knew they had power over them. As they did not come to battle with people but with the dark spirits of the enemy, neither of them showed any fear. This confused Claire, she was used to people being horrified when her dark spirits spoke through her and this scared Claire a bit.

Vicki and Yarran both walked back to Claire who was still hissing and spewing hateful words. The prophets raised their hands to the Father and gave him thanks and praise for guiding them and opening their eyes to the plots of the enemy. They looked at Claire and simply said "Be quiet" The spirits in Claire shuddered and stopped. Still hissing under her breath, Claire was shocked. She thought the evil king was more powerful than anything else but the dark spirits in her were powerless against the spirit, Lord Sabaoth, which just spoke through these prophets. She could feel the fear that her dark spirits felt. Claire decided it might be better if she just shut up.

"Hey, do you hear that? Asked Yarran

"Yeah it sounds like a horse approaching" answered Vicki "It could be more witches, the rest of Claire's coven" she added.

"Nah, I doubt it, we have seen what they think of horses" said Yarran. Vicki repeated her command for the dogs to guard Claire in case she tried something while their attention was on the approaching horse.

They could hear the steady pace of a horse cantering along the track closer and closer. Rhema and Prophet's ears were pricked in the direction of the hoof beats. Even Claire was poised to see what was coming. Rhema let out one of his very loud neighs in excitement and a distant neigh was returned to him.

There was a flash of colour through the thick bush Vicki could just make out a bit of brown. Then from around the corner a man on a beautiful bay appaloosa came into view. The appy had a big white blaze down his face in a very familiar shape like a lightning bolt and a loud blanket of colour over his back right up to his shoulder with big white markings called stockings, up all four legs. He was very flashy. When Vicki and Yarran saw the blaze on the horse they knew it was another prophet approaching them. "Hallelujah" Vicki yelled, Yarran laughed.

The rider slowed to a walk, he pulled up in front of Vicki and Yarran and jumped down from his colourful horse. He was tall with wavy blonde hair and a very nice smile. He was wearing a park ranger uniform.

"G'day, I've been sent by the King to come find two prophets on horseback. Lord Sabaoth guided me here to you, are you who I am looking for?" Then the young man saw the markings on Rhema and prophets foreheads. He laughed "Well that answers that" They all laughed.

Yarran stepped forward and put his hand out to shake saying" G'day mate, I'm Yarran and this is my best mate Vicki" Vicki also shook the man's hand saying"Hi Nice to meet you."

"Hi, I am Isiah, I am a prophet of the King, as you know I'm sure. I work here on the mountain with my little brother Malachi, who is an apostle. We are the park rangers for the entire Yarramundi National Park and this handsome boy is Judge my trusty stead." He said smiling looking at his horse.

"Awesome" said Yarran "always an honour to meet another prophet" he added.

"So, it looks like you have a bit of a situation here, wanna fill me in?" asked Isiah.

"Yeah sure thing" said Yarran as he looked over Judge admiring him, "He's a nice solid boy" said Yarran.

"Ok this is the story" and he started filling Isiah in on everything that had happened on the mountain. He told him about the battles, the Hosts, how they came to be in this spot with Claire and how they suspected that Claire and her coven are responsible for poisoning the water holes in the area.

Siah told Yarran and Vicki how he and Malachi have been fighting to have the law changed and revoke the cull orders and stop the shooting and baiting. But Claire and her coven are part of the law makers on Mt Dominion and the leaders there rule the nation and make the laws. They passed the cull laws to shoot brumby's and bait dingos knowing that the baits will poison other animals and how cruel it is. So because it is a law, they are powerless to stop it. So he and Malachi remove as many bait traps as they can find, and on the days when the choppers are coming to shoot the brumby's they try to heard them into the dense tree cover so the choppers don't see them, but it's not enough we cannot save them all". He explained with great sadness.

"The main thing is you try mate, you can only do your best. It is not on you and your brother nor me and my family. It is on the government and the people that signed off on it." Yarran said with a comforting hand on Siah's shoulder.

Isiah looked up with revelation "Wait! If we can prove those witches have been poisoning water holes, I can take that to court and have them charged. That is not legal, especially in a National park. I can testify to how much devastation they have caused to other wild life not named in the cull order."

"Yarran, can you prove the vial you caught Claire with is the same extract that was used to poison these water holes?" He asked.

"Yep, sure can mate." Yarran was very pleased as he added "My dad kept all the samples we found and I am willing to bet old Claire over there has plenty more of those vials on her."

"Beauty! I will call my brother to come and meet us here to give us a hand, Claire is now in the custody of National parks if she has more vials on her." Said Siah as he grabbed for his radio. Siah called Malachi and asked him to have police waiting for him at the bottom of the mountain and then to come meet them on the track where they were.

He then informed Claire that she was being taken into custody on suspicion of releasing deadly poisons into Natural water ways. That she would be searched and any vials of oleander found on her person would be used against her in court. He secured Claire and Vicki again reaffirmed the stay and guard command with the dogs.

"While we are waiting for Mal to get here, let's go and have a sticky down this track, and see what else old Claire has been up to." Suggested Siah.

Yarran told Siah what he heard Lord Sabaoth say to him about the alter so they approached with caution. Vicki could feel the atmosphere grow heavy and lifeless. She grabbed her shofar and blew. Then all three prophets decreed The Kings authority over the area and took back the territory in the name of The King. Vicki looked up to see Eli and Jelly both take those swords and whoosh off they went, forging the way ahead for the prophets.

Chapter Nine
Hidden Things

The three prophets started down the narrow steep track. They had gone only twenty or so meters before they could see the clearing Lord Sabaoth had warned Yarran about. "That has to be it!" Yarran pointed

to the clearing. They were all preparing themselves for what they might find there. They surged on cautiously, Vicki could see Eli's flashing swords up in the clouds and hear Jelly's rolling thunder. She could feel the battle was winding down it would be a sweet victory when these rulers of darkness are dethroned and then the wicked people at the top doing their bidding are unseated and taken to justice. Then The King's children, can finally take their rightful place on top of this mountain and eventually all seven mountains of the Kingdom.

The prophets finally came to the mouth of the clearing, they could see it was a circle of land made void of trees and cleared of all shrub. There were weird markings and symbols everywhere carved into wooden statues. In the centre of the circle was a large bed of rocks piled on one another. It was also circular, large and flat at the top.

"Well, well, well, someone has been busy here, haven't they? They have broken so many laws to do all this. All flora and fauna is protected in a nation park even the rocks. But the removal of trees will get you gaol time. So we can take them into custody for that, for sure." Declared Siah with a grin.

"I guess it's better than nothing, but they are not going to admit to it" added Vicki.

"Don't worry." Siah reassured Vicki. "We caught Claire red handed so unless she wants to cop all these charges on her own and receive maximum penalties, she will talk and if she does talk, we will go a little easier on her."

This made both Vicki and Yarran smile. "She might be working with the elites of this mountain but we work for a higher power." Proclaimed Vicki.

"Amen." Decreed Siah and Yarran.

"Come on, we will search around until Mal gets here. But don't touch anything no matter how disturbing it might be. We will need to come back and photograph everything."

"Ok Siah, no worries." Agreed Yarran.

Vicki felt Lord Sabaoth was leading her down a track that was somewhat obscured by the bushes at the circles edge. She slowly walked along a rocky path looking out for snakes as she went as they like to warm themselves on rocks and love undisturbed areas of rocks that get heated by sun's rays. She continued on a few more meters when she noticed another path that was off to the side. This path looked well-worn so Vicki went to investigate. She had gone about fifty metres when she heard a sound. Vicki stopped immediately and listened "What was that?" she asked Lord Sabaoth. Then she heard it again, it was the sobbing voice of a woman.

"Guys over here!" she yelled as loud as she could. Yarran and Siah both took off as fast as they could in the direction of Vicki's voice. "Vicky, where are you?" Yarran called out at the top of his lungs.

"I am down a path to the left of the alter. Hurry, someone is down here." She cried.

Just then the voice called out. "Help, Help me please, Hello, Hello is there anyone out there." "Please Father, please send them to help me." The voice rang out and echoed down the mountain track.

"Hello, Yes I am here, keep calling so I can find you." Vicki answered.

"Oh thank you Father" the voice called out with sounds of relief. "I am in here, I am locked in the cave over here." The woman continued until Vicki saw what looked like something concealed by branches and the woman's voice was coming from behind them. So Vicki quickly started removing the ones she could manage. "It's OK, I am here, I found you." Vicki tried to reassure the woman.

Yarran and Siah came tearing up to Vicki. "What is it Vicki?"

"There is a woman trapped in here. Come and help me get these branches out of the way." She cried.

The guys started pulling the branches off the opening until Siah stopped. "Wait, she could be one of them? So be careful, they turn on each other all the time."

"I don't think so, I heard her crying out and thanking the Father for us finding her and it was Lord Sabaoth that led me to her. I think Father used us to answer her prayers." Informed Vicki.

"Please help me, please get me out." The sobbing voice cried out again.

"Yes we are almost there just a couple more branches." Answered Vicki.

When the last big branch was pulled away. The prophets could not believe what they were seeing. It was the opening to what seemed like a cave at first glance, the mouth of it was sealed with big steel bars and a gate that was padlocked.

Siah was stunned at this find. "I grew up on this mountain and have worked here ten years I've studied every inch and know where every cave is, this is not supposed to be here." He looked on in amazement. Then he shone his torch into the mouth of the cave. "This isn't like any other cave I have ever seen." He said.

"Wait, what was that over on the right?" asked Yarran. "I saw something reflect."

Siah shone his torch back to the right it looked like metal bars.

"Hello!" called Vicki. "It is OK, we will help you, don't be afraid."

"I am here!" Cried the woman. "I am waiving my arms through the bars." She said.

Siah pointed his torch directly on the bars and sure enough there was an arm waiving at them.

"Oh my gosh, we have to get her out." Exclaimed Vicki, horrified at the thought of the poor woman trapped in a place such as this. The woman started crying, relieved Father had sent help. She was crying and thanking her rescuers.

"We will have you out of there in no time." Yarran reassured her, then examining the chain and padlock, he looked at Siah.

"This is a pretty serious lock, we will have to cut the chains, don't suppose you have bolt cutters on you?"

"No I don't." Answered Siah. "I do have a heavy duty hammer and chisel for breaking rocks open? I am an amateur gemmologist. It's my hobby."

"I will go get them, I think I can break the padlock." He added as he headed back to judge to get them from his saddle bags. "I will check on Claire while I am there." He yelled back as he disappeared through the bush.

Meanwhile, Vicki and Yarran kept their attention on the woman trapped in the cave. "I am Vicki, this is my best friend Yarran"

"Hi and Siah is the one that just ran off to get something to open this lock." Yarran replied.

"Oh thank you Father," the woman sobbed

"What is your name?" "Vicki Asked.

"My name is "Daphne, everyone calls me Daf." Answered the woman.

"Oh that is a pretty name, Daf are you hurt at all?" asked Vicki.

"No, I have not eaten in three days though, but I am ok, I just need to get word to my family that I am alright before they sell everything we own to save me." She revealed.

Vicki and Yarran just looked at each other. That was a strange statement. They thought perhaps she maybe dehydrated and confused.

"Oh Daf, as soon as we get you out you can use Siah's radio and ask police to let your family know. Unfortunately there is not much phone signal this side of the mountain." Vicki explained.

"I know, I worked on top of the mountain at the big media network." Daf went on, "You can get a text out, could you please send one to my husband James? Just to let him know you have found me and to expect the police to ring. Please, it is important and I will explain everything." She pleaded.

"OK, sure I can do that. What is James's number?" Asked Vicki. Daf gave Vicki, James's number and dictated what she wanted Vicki to say. It went... Hello James, I am Vicki. I am here with a National Park Ranger, we have found your wife Daphne. We are in the process of freeing her, but she wanted me to let you know. Do Not sell anything, I am ok and will be home soon. Please expect a call from the police today.

Vicki had no idea what exactly that meant but sent it anyway to comfort Daf. "OK sent" Said Vicki.

"Oh thank you so much." Replied Daf, she went on "I know it must sound crazy, I will explain but first I..." Daf was interrupted by Siah bursting through the bushes and announcing that Mal was with him.

Mal was tall and slender with fine brown hair and big brown eyes. He smiled and said "Hi, you must be Vicki and Yarran, Siah filled me in with what is going on."

"Hi Mal." Said Vicki.

"G'day Mal, nice to meet you. You don't happen to have a pair of bolt cutters do you?" Asked Yarran.

"Nah, sorry mate, Siah is going to chisel the lock off." He answered.

"I have them here, Yarran hold the lock for me." Asked Siah as he began clanking the hammer down on the chisel against the padlock. "Now if I hit it in just the right spot it should pop open... In theory." He explained as he continued smashing the hammer down as hard as he could.

"You got it, good going Siah." Yarran exclaimed as he threw the popped lock to the ground and started pulling the chain through the bars. "Ok, we are in." He cried.

"We are coming in Daf, sit tight we will come and get you." Vicki called out into the darkness in front of her.

"Ok, please hurry, I cannot stand it in here." Cried Daphne.

With torches blazing, Siah and Mal forged their way through the dark cavern to the bars they caught site of earlier. The bars were part of a large cage big enough to fit ten people, with a ledge calved out in the wall for a seat. There in the corner hunched over hiding her eyes from the bright torch light was Daphne. She was a pitiful sight. Her hair was matted and she was covered in dirt. Weak from dehydration and no food. Vicki gently walked over to her and said. "Hi Daphne, it's nice to put a face to the voice. Let me help you up, slowly does it now."

Yarran slowly walked over to the other side and gently spoke to her as he took her other arm to help her up. "Hi Daphne, I am Yarran."

The prophets helped her to walk outside and get some fresh air and sunlight. They sat her down on a rock and gave her some water, while Siah and Mal continued looking through the cave.

They both came out shaking their heads and Siah bent down to grab the padlock for evidence. "Guys do not touch anything else."

He announced." This is now a crime scene and police will have to be involved. That is no cave, it's a tunnel."

He then walked over to Daphne and said "Hi Daphne, I am Isiah. I am a ranger in this park, could I ask you a few questions just to help us understand what has happened here?"

Daphne broke down in tears. "Yes". She sobbed.

"Ok, how did you come to be locked in the cave and who put you there?" He asked.

"It's a long story." She said. As she took another sip of water and gathered her strength to explain. "I was a high up executive, working up the top of this mountain for Metface. Life was good, I was well paid and I loved my job. My family have a nice house in a good neighbourhood and my kids go to a good school.

A few months ago at work I started noticing new policies coming across my desk from the high ups. About new censorship guidelines we were to put in place for the algorithms. I signed off on them at first and I went along with the changes believing it was for the good of the people. I thought we were putting out the truth about this pandemic and other current issues including a new vaccine, though it was untested it was deemed to be safe. These new policies would censure the other narratives some people were posting.

There was a lot of negative things being posted calling these Government mandates false and misleading the people. They were against all the mandates such as wearing masks and social distancing and especially this new vaccination - trying to stop people from taking it and saying it was unsafe. We were told that these were lies, false information put out by over the top conspiracy groups." So these new policies seemed a good thing.

"After a while though I became aware we were censoring every private post and even other political leader's posts. Basically anyone that went against the main narrative. Even though they were respected members of community. Then I saw countless medical professionals who dared to speak out against this vaccine get cancelled and threatened to have their medical license revoked if they did not keep silent. It seemed they

          Saving the Second Kingdom

wanted to take the right to choose away from everyone. Some doctors refused to give into this blackmail and were cancelled. This made me think... hang on, something just isn't right here."

"I couldn't work out what until I overheard a conversation one day just outside my office door. There was a big conference to be held that day. It was very hush, hush. The CEO of Metface, Dork Suckaburger and Phil Bates the CEO of Craple, part of a small elite group pushing for governments to force people to take this medicine, were meeting with Cloth Swobs another elite pushing his reset agenda.

It was very secretive and no one was allowed on the conference floor while this was happening. However, the staff they had brought with them were getting water just outside my office door and I overheard them talking about all the people being under a spell that put them into a sleep state so they do not question the story of lies they are fed.

It all started years ago by putting fluoride in the water supply. They found that it affects a part of your brain that makes you more agreeable. Then they were discussing how effective using movies, music, music videos, social media and social groups with initials instead of names were to help put in place their wicked plans and break down the morals of society. They attacked the family unit first,"

"The biggest secret behind it all, the thing they do not want you to know... is this is all to worship of Baal. I heard them say. They boasted about sacrifices they performed and the suffering of people that they had caused in the name of Baal.

It all hit me a like a brick, the cruelly the callousness towards us all. They spoke of us like we were cattle."

"My head was reeling from what I just heard, I thought I was going to throw up. My first reaction was, I have to tell someone. I waited for those people to leave and I went to find my friend, Claire. I thought I could trust her, well that was my first mistake." Daphne paused momentarily she put her head in her hands and sobbed.

Vicki sat down beside her and placed her arm around her for support. Vicki reached for the water bottle. "Here Daf, have a little more water, take your time." She said gently. Then Vicky spoke over

Daf. "Father I place Daphne and her family in your loving hands and I ask you to give them the strength they will need to get through the next few days. Please remove any trauma from their souls. I ask in the name of The King."

When Vicki had finished. Daf thanked her and said. "I am ok now I can continue."

"So when I went to Claire and confided in her all that I just overheard, Claire seemed shocked and started saying, this could be dangerous. That we should not tell just anyone as we do not know who else is in on it and how high up the corruption goes. Not to say anything to family or friends as I could be putting them in danger." Daf stopped and said "This made sense to me and then I felt bad for telling Claire." She continued "So I agreed to keep quiet and I apologised to Claire for putting her in jeopardy."

"The next day I went to work as usual, trying to act normal like nothing had happened and there on my desk were promotion papers. I had been after this executive position for years but was always told I would never get it as I was under qualified but I knew I was totally qualified. So I figured it was a boys club or something."

"The promotion came with a pay rise but the offer on my desk was doubled what it actually should have been. When I saw the promotion I did get excited and a little puzzled, but when I saw how much more money they were offering me, my stomach turned. I knew instantly that it was a bribe to keep my mouth shut and then it hit me. The only soul that I told was Claire."

"I felt sick, my head started swimming. I felt very exposed and scared for my life. All I could think of was 'I have to get out of here'. So I made an excuse to my secretary saying I had left some very important papers at home that I needed to go and get. I got out of there as fast as I could, but I wasn't fast enough apparently. Claire and two big goons I had never seen before were waiting for me at my car."

"It turns out that my 'Good friend' Claire is a very wicked person. She is part of a horrible dark cult and she is so not who she pretended to be."

                    Saving the Second Kingdom

"They gave me one more chance to take the job offer to which I declined. The next thing I was tied up and thrown in the back of a van and this is where they brought me. I overheard them plotting to destroy my family." Daphne started sobbing. "Claire was saying how she would make this look like a random kid napping and ask for a ransom that is so high that James would have to sell everything we owned just to pay it. Once he had paid, they were going to sell me to another country as a slave in a sweatshop anyway. My family would have nothing and I would never see them again. 'Madness! '" Daf exclaimed. "Pure madness, these people are insane." She sobbed.

"When they finally left I was terrified, it was so dark inside there and so quiet and I was so alone. I was desperate for my family. Then a child hood memory popped into my head of the time my nana took me to her church. I remember hearing about The Father and how The King had willingly sacrificed himself to save us and give us all a way back to Him. So for the first time in my life I got down on my knees and started begging The Father for help. As I did so I was filled with a beautiful feeling, I have never felt so much peace. I told The Father that if he would save me and my family, I would turn my life around and live for him. For three days now they have kept me in that cell waiting for James to come up with the ransom money". Daphne broke down again, knowing how much her family must be suffering.

"Daf" Vicki said as she put her hand on Daf's shoulder. "We were led here to you by our dogs who are a very special gift from Father, and Lord Sabaoth himself led me to that little hidden track over there." Vicki pointed to the track to the left of the Alter. "I just wanted you to know Daf that we are prophets of The King most high and Father did answer your prayer. He guided us here right to you. He is real, He is so very good and He loves you beyond measure." Vicki added with a heartfelt smile.

"I know" confessed Daf "He is real, I could feel him in that cell with me the whole time. It was so comforting. He was speaking to me in my spirit. He is the only reason I am still sane and able to talk about it." She wept tears of joy and then said "When I get home, my family and I will be surrendering our hearts to the King and living our lives as He would want us to."

"That's great news Hallelujah" they all cheered. Vicki looked up and could see thousands of angels dancing, singing and rejoicing. She wondered what they were celebrating. She heard Lord Sabaoth say "This is what happens in my Kingdom when one of my lost children return to Me."

"Wow, that's awesome." Vicki said to herself realizing she was the only one that was seeing this. Then Siah's voice broke the momentary silence, "OK, Mal did you put that call into the police?"

"Yep, sure did, they should be waiting at the gate on the entrance road."

"Oh Good." Said Siah.

"Can I get you to take care of Daphne while I deal with our 'friend' Claire? I have a sneaking feeling good old Claire just may have the key to this padlock on her."

"Yeah no probs." Answered Mal.

"Let's go find Claire." Added Yarran.

The five of them made their way back to where they had left the dogs and Claire. As they drew closer, there began to hear Claire's scratchy voice cursing at the dogs. This made them laugh. "You guys make sure to give those two dogs a big treat when you get home for putting up with old Claire so patiently." Siah said laughing.

"Hi Claire." Said Yarran. "We found a friend of yours while we were investigating your little dungeon setup you have." He revealed.

"That is no friend of mine, I have never seen her before." Claire started to protest. "You should stay out of that place, I hear bad things happen to people that interfere with a place like that."

Vicki laughed at Claire and gave her some food for thought. "Well Claire, you may worship baal and think he is all powerful, but to me, you are looking at a pot and giving it praise when really it's the potter that should receive the praise for their works. Is it not? Well I worship the potter in this case. Mull that over in your corrupted mind as we take

Saving the Second Kingdom

you down the mountain and hand you over to the waiting police." Vicki added "Remember with The Father it is never too late for anyone to repent and change their ways Claire, even you."

Siah told Claire that she would have to be searched and asked Vicki if she would do the honours. Vicki searched Claire thoroughly and in a hidden inside pocket found a single key on its own. "I bet this is the key to the padlock." She said as she continued searching. Then from the outside coat pocket she found a plastic bag full of those gel vials Claire had tried to poison Prophet with. Vicki showed them to Yarran straight away.

"Huh" Said Yarran.

"I knew it, there you go Siah and I bet those will match the samples we have at home."

"Yep so do I." Agreed Siah. "Now for the key!" He put it in the lock and turned it to hear a click and the lock opened.

"Well, well." Said Siah as he handed the padlock to Mal and told him to put everything in evidence bags sealed properly for the police.

"Looks like you will have quite a few serious charges on you Claire. I think you're the one who better ring your family and let them know you will not be home for a while." Siah said with a grin of satisfaction.

Vicki and Yarran wished Daf a safe return to her family. "If you are looking for a good group of people to get to know Father better, find Paul the Evangelist. He will point you in the right direction. Just look for a huge tent down on the creek flats and the Holden Ute with the lightning bolt." Laughed Vicki.

"I cannot thank you both enough for being so obedient to Lord Sabaoth's leading you here, even though it took you away from your mission." Daf said with tears rolling down her cheeks.

Vicki interjected "Daf, you were our mission."

Daf continued. "I have written down my phone number and address. Please give me a ring when you are done on this mountain, so we can get together and give you all a proper thank you."

"That is not necessary." Said Vicki. "We were merely the vessels, thank The Father. Give all praise and glory to him. We are just doing what we were created to do, but we would love to come and meet James and the children."

"Fantastic they would love to meet you too." Replied Daf.

Siah and Mal shook hands with Vicki and Yarran. Siah thanked them for everything, they exchanged numbers as they knew they would be needed for the court cases. Vicki and Yarran wished them well and the Ranges turned and started the long trek down the mountain to the entrance of the National Park.

"Come on Vicki, let's setup camp for the night. It has been a long day." Yawned Yarran.

Chapter Ten
When Judgment Comes

As dawns first light peeked through the tree tops. Vicki and Yarran set off for the top of the mountain. Lightning streaked through the morning sky with rolling thunder behind. The prophets watched the dark cloud as the light show continued, every now and then they caught a glimpse of a wing or a sword wielding arm. The battle raged on and it's seemed more intense. Vicki grabbed her shofar and Yarran spoke victory over the battle. Vicki commanded all the powers and principalities over the mountain evicted in the name of The King, she bound them in chains for the angel to come and drag them away.

"The battle seems really intense today Vicki." Yarran said.

"Yeah, I think it is because we are nearly to the top of the mountain and the Hosts are now battling the principalities raining over the mountain, having defeated all of their army." She answered. "Keep decreeing victory, let's give the Hosts plenty to fight with." She added as she blew her shofar again.

"I wonder how Isiah and Mal went with Claire and Daf! I hope Claire turns her life around for Father!" Said Vicki.

"Yeah me too Vicki, I bet Daf's family are celebrating today. Laughed Yarran.

"Yeah I hope so, they deserve to celebrate." Agreed Vicki. "I hope Daf finds Paul too, so he can help her to get to know The Father and introduce her family to him." Sighed Vicki.

"Hey the track looks fairly clear for a bit, lets pick up the pace while we can." Suggested Yarran. He whistled for Logos and Preacher to keep up as they cantered off at a steady pace. They cantered along the track for a few hundred metres and they came to an abrupt halt. An old tree had come down across the track, completely blocking their way. The sides of the mountain were too steep to go around and the branches were way too high to jump over.

"Ahh, there is no way around it, we are going to need help." Said Yarran as he dismounted to investigate further. Standing on the fallen tree he could see the track ahead for a short distance. "Looks like a

Saving the Second Kingdom

hard slog from here. It's all rocks and boulders covering the track," He called out.

"Wait a minute." Cried Vicki. "Father warned us of this. He told us that once we get close to the top, the enemy will perceive us a threat and try to put up road blocks to distract us and discourage us."

She jumped down from Rhema and walked up to the tree and said "We need The King to make a way for us. He is the way maker!" She got down on her knees, humbled herself and called on The King. "In The Name of The King, I command this mountain to be shaken, this tree to be dislodged and I decree a pathway to open up for us to travel on, let this be done as it is in His Kingdom."

Then Vicki took her whip from around her shoulder and cracked it. Knowing it symbolised the shield of faith in the natural. The crack from the stock whip echoed in ripples down through the trees. Then there was a rumble in the ground, it felt like it came from the very core of the mountain and a flurry of wind blew in all around them like a whirlwind. Vicki and Yarran who were both thanking The King opened their eyes and were amazed. A company of beautiful angels were causing the ground to shake to remove the obstacles from the path of the prophets.

Once the path was clear, the angels just seemed to vanish. They both spent time thanking The King and talking with The Father still marvelling at what they had both just seen and so grateful of their Father's love and grace. Seeing this had renewed their spirits and energised them so they could carry on.

"Come on, let's make up for lost time." Said Yarran as he climbed up on Prophet. "We can reach the top by noon if we keep a steady pace."

"Yep let's go." Agreed Vicki.

She blew her shofar as they started back along the track.

Just as Vicki blew her shofar. A huge single crack of thunder rang out, it was so loud it shook the ground and brought Vicki and Yarran to instant stop.

"Whoa, that was huge!" proclaimed Yarran.

"Look!" Cried Vicki pointing to the huge dark cloud that had been looming over the mountain and valley's since the pandemic started.

It was like someone had ripped it in two and for the first time in two years, rays of sunlight penetrated through the break and lit up the valley below, it was almost blinding. It was so bright so suddenly. Like being in a dark room and someone turning the light on without warning.

Vicki couldn't help wondering if all the people living below were witnessing this too, or if they were the only ones seeing this through their gift of spiritual sight.

Lord Sabaoth answered her and said "No, to the people in the valley's below it looks and sounds like a big storm brewing, but to the people at the top of the mountain, they are very scared and want to scatter like rats on a sinking ship. They know they are about to face judgement for their many crimes. Many will turn on each other and confess to their crimes in hopes of leniency from the courts. Some will try to run but will find no place to hide. Then there will be those who hearts will fail them as I allow them all to witness my mighty armies defeat their false gods."

"I gave them chance after chance to stop their wicked ways and turn to me for mercy and forgiveness, but they hardened their hearts and turned their backs to me and continued down their path to destruction. I could ignore the cries of my children no more."

"I will usher in a new day on Earth. Never before seen. I am doing a new thing, this is 'My' great reset and My children will rejoice and celebrate. They will have greater power to do more signs and wonders than ever before. My children will enjoy freedom and prosperity, the likes of which have never been seen on Earth. I will pour out my glory over the Earth and The King will take his rightful place on Earth. Millions of my children shall find their way back to me. There shall be peace and prosperity on the Earth."

As Lord Sabaoth spoke these words to Vicki, he showed her a vision so that she could see and understand how good life was about to be. This filled Vicki's heart with hope and gave her renewed

Saving the Second Kingdom

strength to forge ahead. She could now see the future they were fighting for.

"Yarran, I must tell you what Lord Sabaoth just told me." She yelled with such excitement, she instantly had Yarran's attention. She told him all about what Lord Sabaoth just said and what it would look like. This penetrated Yarran's spirit and filled him with a renewed strength also.

Together they were both ready for anything the enemy may throw at them. They had been given a glimpse of their victory in The King. They both sent out decrees with even more fire in their faith.

There was a huge jolt in the air, the prophets both felt it. It was shift in the spiritual atmosphere followed by rolling thunder throughout the vast clouds. The prophets knowingly smiled at the now familiar sound. There was another shift that could be felt in the natural and a ripping sound like the tearing away of fabric. The great cloud was breaking up into seven smaller clouds. Instantly, Vicki had revelation that there was one cloud representing each of the seven mountains on Earth and that one by one they will now be taken back from the enemy. As they looked on, the seven clouds started to spread further part. One staying directly above mount Yarramundi.

"We are nearly there Vicki, I saw buildings through the tree tops." Cried Yarran.

"Grab your shofar, let's declare this mountain belonging to The King. Under covenant with The Father we now take this mountain back under the control of the King's ecclesia." Declared Vicki.

They both blew their shofars and made decrees as they pressed on as fast as the horses could navigate the step path.

A thunderous roar penetrated the entire sky above, then followed by sharp crack of thunder. It sounded as if the heavens themselves had split open. A portal appeared in the sky and then began to suck up the portion of the black cloud directly above mount Yarramundi until the sky was a beautiful clear bright blue above.

The prophets were stopped on a cliff face, looking on amazed and thrilled to bits.

"They've done it." Vicki announced. "They have won the battle." Referring to Eli and his Hosts. "Let's go, we are almost at the top." She yelled trotting off on Rhema.

A gust of wind picked up and swirled around them like a protective barrier. The prophets were in wonder, then the wind became visible. It was Eli, Jelly and the rest of the battalion they all had big smiles on their faces. "Allow us to escort you the rest of the way" said Eli. As they tightened formation around Vicki and Yarran.

"Praise The King for victory, praise The King!" Vicki shouted. Raising her shofar like a sword above her head.

"Here, Here." Shouted the Hosts.

Then Eli shouted "Three cheers to The King. Hooray, hooray, hooray!" They all rejoiced in the victory over the rulers of darkness, up high in the second heaven and the defeat of the powers and principalities that were under their command and rained over mount Yarramundi.

"Now, to remove the corrupt leaders and laws in the natural." Declared Yarran.

"Yeah, let's go finish this." Cried Vicki.

So they carried on up the steepest part of the track. Two prophets of The King, their horses and two dogs, surrounded by a battalion of host angels with a commander of the royal guard leading them. It was a sight to behold.

As they approached the top Eli swung back to speak to the young prophets. "Remember." He said. "Father has opened the eyes of the wicked. Only, the wicked, no one else who works there. So all the unrepentant souls will see us and they will see you in your true form dressed in the amour of The Father. So they may act and react as if they are seeing a ghost." Eli said with a grin. He went on. "Father wants them to see that they are on the wrong path that will lead them to their own destruction. He does not want any of his children to perish. Seeing us will lead some of them to repent and turn back from the dark path they have chosen."

"Ok Eli, we understand, all glory to The King." Answered Yarran.

"Glory to Yahweh. Holy, Holy, Holy, is His name!" The whole battalion of Hosts cried out.

They continued along the ascending track until they came to a plateau. "The top is just around the next corner." Announced Eli.

The two prophets readied themselves for anything. Not knowing how the people would react to the sight of two royal knights in armour coming towards them surrounded by a whirlwind of angelic Hosts. The Hosts themselves are very confronting.

They rounded the corner and it was like stepping into another world. They literally stepped out of the bush track and onto a tarred road with streets and buildings. It was like a world of its own. The two prophets rode down the middle of the road, the sounds of the horses shoes echoed off the buildings and seemed amplified. They got half way down the main street when Lord Sabaoth spoke to them. "Stop here prophets and call out the wicked and corrupted ones."

Vicki and Yarran dismounted and drew their swords from their scabbards. They held them up above their heads, hilt and handle up, tip pointing to the ground. Vicki spoke out in the authority given to her by The King. "It is written, woe to those that call evil good and good evil, who replace darkness with light, and light with darkness, who replace bitter with sweet and sweet with bitter. For they said 'No!' to the teachings of Yahweh, the Lord of Angel armies and have despised the word of the holy one of Israel!"

Then Yarran spoke in his authority from The King. "We come against you in the name of Lord Almighty, The God of the armies of Israel whom you have defied. You uncircumcised philistines. This day The Lord will hand you over to us and you shall be struck down."

Both the prophets readied their swords and as they thrust them straight down into the ground, they called "Come out now!"

When the swords hit the ground, it made a loud boom and a shockwave was released. Its ripples expanded out from the swords, encircling the entire area. Every building was engulfed in the ripples of the wave. Then the ground under them began to shake. It shook every building in its circumference.

The prophets stood unshaken in their faith, swords to the ground, as people came pouring out from every building screaming and scurrying, fearing an earthquake.

At first they did not notice the two royal Knights and a battalion of Hosts standing in formation behind them, they were too gripped with fear to notice. As more and more people came filing out of the buildings the streets became more crowded and though there was screaming from the panic as people were running out, there began to be ear piercing shrieks of pure fear like a wild boar caught in a snare. These were the screams of the unrighteous as they caught sight of the army waiting to bring them their harvest for their years of sowing evil seeds.

Above all the screams and commotion, there was another wailing scream off in the distance.

"Can you hear that?" Asked Vicki.

"What is that?" She asked.

Yarran strained to hear over the crowd now lining the streets.

"I am not sure, but I think it's sirens" he answered.

"Eli." Vicki called. "Take the battalion and gather the wicked ones to the left side of the street to make it easier to deal with them. Do what you must to get them to obey, but they must not leave here. Place chains of justice on the ones that refuse to comply or try to run."

In a flash, Eli and the Hosts were in amongst the crowds carrying out Vicki's command.

Meanwhile the sirens were getting louder.

"It sounds like they are coming here." Said Yarran.

"Yeah, I think they are." Agreed Vicki.

The Hosts had the crowds sorted, they had the corrupted and wicked on the left side of the street and all other employees and visitors on the right side. By now the sirens were very close and the prophets could tell it wasn't just one, it sounded like many.

"Could they be coming here?" Vicki asked Yarran, puzzled.

"Well it sounds like it, and that makes sense, this will be their judgment coming for their many crimes against the Nations." Answered Yarran.

Saving the Second Kingdom

The police cars came into view as they rounded the last corner. First one, followed by another until there were ten police cars in a line all with lights flashing and sirens wailing.

The prophets lifted their swords and placed them back in their scabbards. Then they stretched out their hands and said. "Be still." Commanding the earth to stop shaking.

The police shut off their sirens and made their way slowly like a motorcade to where the prophets and their horses stood. They came to a stop and the back doors of the first police car flung open. The prophets watched on with intrigue to see who was about to get out.

A pair of riding boots appeared as they slapped down onto the tar. Then a head popped up, it was Isiah and Mal jumped out from the other side. Siah turned extending his arm into the car again and out hopped Daphne. The prophets were delighted to see their friends. They both ran to greet them and couldn't wait to hear to what had happened to bring them back with the police.

Vicki called out "Oh gosh it's great to see you guys, you obviously made it down the mountain."

As she ran to greet them, shrieks of terror filled the air. They all looked over to the left side of the street. There were two men that thought they could escape the judgment looming over them while Vicki and Yarran were distracted. They were stopped by two huge angels with massive chains. The men, terrified, screaming as these angels secured them with the chains. They had no choice but to wait where they stood for the police to come and arrest them.

Vicki and Yarran chuckled at this site and they noticed that Siah and Mal were as well and to their surprise so were some of the police.

"Can you see that?" Yarran asked Siah.

"Yes, I now have the gift of spiritual site, so does Mal and it looks like a couple of the cops here are seers to."

"Yeah, I notice that too." Said Yarran.

"It is quite a site to see guys, let me tell you. You look good in armour." Laughed Mal.

"Daphne, it's so good to see you. But I thought you would be home catching up with your family." Said Vicki.

"James was waiting for me at the bottom of the mountain. So I did get to see him briefly but I have been giving my statement to the police and they had a doctor check me over. The police wanted me here in case they needed me to confirm anyone's I.D. or direct involvement in my abduction." Daf answered.

"Well, you look much better now, I am glad." Added Yarran.

The police had lined everyone up and were systematically going through their list of employees and making arrests. Others were allowed to leave, but had to report to the station for their statements to be taken.

Then the police came to the men frozen in chains. The men were trembling with such fear, they almost handcuffed themselves to get away from the angels. The arresting officers thought they were scared of them as only a few could see what was actually happening. The men all but told them to hurry up and get them in the car. They went to walk but were still stuck. The angels wanted them to see Fathers power is much greater than their baal or any other false god they knew. It was not until the angels released them with one word "Go" could they move. One of the angels bent down - as he was about fourteen feet high - and said "it's not too late to repent and change your ways." To one of those men who turned out to be the CEO and the most wicked of all. Both men now cowering and shuttered in terror with the angel bending down over them. The police that had hold of their arms both looked puzzled and said. "I think we should do a drug test on these two."

The CEO started yelling. "We are not on drugs. Don't you see the giants with wings and the chains? Is this a setup? What is wrong with you?" He was yelling all the way to the back of the squad car. Vicki, Yarran, Siah, Mal and Daf couldn't help themselves, they were in hysterics. Though Daf couldn't see, the prophets had described the entire scene to her.

As the police cars pulled away loaded with criminals. One car came around the corner towards them and pulled up right next to them.

"Oh its James cried Daf." With surprise. "He did say he wanted to meet you guys."

A tall, well dressed, nice looking man got out of the car and very cautiously walked over towards them. His mouth gapped open and he was surveying the entire scene. The prophets knew from the look on his face, He was seeing the entire scene.

"James!" Daf cried with excitement as she ran to greet her husband. "Come meet these guys."

Daf had James by the hand pulling him to walk faster.

"Vicki, Yarran, This is my husband James." Daf announced.

James hugged Vicki and shook Yarrans hand. "I cannot begin to tell you how grateful my family is to you both, to you all." He said gesturing with his arms as to include Siah and Mal as well.

"We would have been financially ruined and would have seen Daf again. It's so scary how close we came to losing her forever. I will always considering you all family. We will be forever in your debt." He said with a quivering chin.

All four warriors spoke in spontaneous agreement. "No James please you don't owe us anything, there is no debt to pay and no thanks needed for us, we are servants of The King most high. It was Lord Sabaoth that saved your Daf. He is the one that led us to her. It is our Father and The King you should thank."

"Well I thank you for your obedience to The Father, I knew The Father as a boy, and I gave my heart to The King when I was just five years old. My mother is a believer, but I strayed away when I hit my teenage years. Not anymore, we will be going back to The Father and joining in on this war in whatever way he needs us to.

"James that is fantastic news." Yarran said.

"And I have some news for you Daf." Interjected Vicki. "Lord Sabaoth just gave me a word for you. You belong on the mountain of education but also on this mountain, Mount Yarramundi, the mountain of media.

He wants you to be in charge of the entire mountain and to teach everyone that will work under you the ways of The Father. First though he will train you and teach you and will raise you up in faith if you will allow him. Thus say the word of The Lord."

"Me? He wants 'Me' to be at the top?" Daf blurted out in shock and awe.

Vicki laughed "Yes Daf, you proved to The Father that you can be trusted by saying no to corruption even when it threatened your family. He wants to reward you for that and he wants you to join us in raising up an army of righteous to lead, not just this Nation but all Nations. You will be in charge of leading and training many in the ways of righteousness and truth. You will oversee this mountain and bring thousands into His Kingdom."

Vicki added with great delight and then turned to James and said "James, I have a word for you to. Thus say The Lord this day, James you have been true and loving to your family and by this you have honoured me, you have a heart for my people. I have given you spiritual site this day and will put you at the top of this mountain next to my daughter Daphne. You will not be parted from her again. You shall be a watchmen for this mountain and bring it about that families shall come to work here in a family friendly environment catering for the needs of all from schools to fitness, so that no family on this mountain will be apart every day."

"I am deeply honoured, wow, that is amazing, and I cannot wait to get started." Declared James.

By Now the last of the criminals had been removed and only the forensic team remained. Eli appeared and announced that they have an appointment with the Commander and Chief. This made James jump, Eli was very intimidating to see. "I'm going to have to get used to this new sight" James laughed with his hand still over his heart from fright. Eli smiled at James and said "You will, don't worry. You will have Angelic Hosts assigned to you very soon." He smiled again and bowed his head at James and with that, Eli and the battalion of Hosts were gone. All that remained was a beautiful silver feather that

Saving the Second Kingdom

floated down and landed at James' feet. He bent down and picked it up.

"Looks like Eli likes you James, His feather is his offer of friendship" Vicki remarked, leaving James utterly speechless.

"Well guys it's time for us to get going, we have a long ride home but we will stay in contact. Let's meet at Paul's tent on Sunday morning" suggested Yarran

"Yes that's a great idea" agreed Daf.

Then Siah spoke, "Daf Lord Sabaoth has just told me that I am to be your assigned prophet and Mal will be the apostle assigned to you. To give you guidance and help establish this mountain for the Kingdom. So we will be working together with you." Daf was elated to hear this.

Vicki and Yarran said goodbye and mounted their horses. Siah and Mal asked James for a lift back to the ranger's station. Yarran whistled for logos and Preacher to come and they slowly rode away.

Watching till they were out of sight, everyone else piled into James car and drove down the now deserted road.

Vicki and Yarran were slowly meandering back down the steep track. They continued until they reached the last plateau that they stopped at on the way up, where they had watched the Hosts defeat the enemy in high places. They decided it would be a good idea to camp there for the night and get a fresh start early in the morning.

They unsaddled the horses and set up their swags for the night. Yarran gave the dogs some dried meat and some water. Then they both sat in silence listening to the horses happily chomping on the native grasses, as they reflected back over the last few days and all that had transpired.

A voice broke through the silence, it sounded like a hundred waterfalls cascading over them, it said" My prophets come up here." Both Vicki and Yarran knew it was the voice of their beloved King and in that instance a portal opened before them. They could see a brilliant white light emanating from the centre and the King spoke to them again "Come my prophets, my children, come let me show you what is next".

Vicki and Yarran were mesmerised by the beauty that laid before them when they stepped through the portal and into an open field of splendour they could never have imagined.

The air smelled sweet like jasmine and orange blossoms, the grass was like emerald crystals, light seemed to pass through it, yet not. It had a life of its own. As they scanned the beautiful scene in front of them, they were speechless and in awe. The clouds billowed like pure white cotton. The water in the stream seemed to be like liquid crystal, it sparkled like diamonds and had beautiful gemstones of all colours through it, yet it was flowing like water. Everything was teaming with life and everything was full of life abundant.

In the middle of the field stood a glorious tree whose branches stretched out far and wide and its leaves sparkled in the perfect white light. The tree had a life of its own, as it moved and reacted. It was the most gorgeous tree.

Under it stood the Father and The King. They were dressed in the finest robes. They both had long white tunics with long sleeves having gold embroidery around the collar and cuffs and were adorned with beautiful purple and gold sashes. The King had a glorious golden crown on his head studded with gemstones neither prophet had seen before and it had words inscribed on it. It was magnificent.

They were surprised to see Rhema and Logos, Prophet and Preacher waiting there for them beside the King. Both horses had beautiful golden blankets, each with its own intricate patterns all around the edges, just so ornate. The dogs were adored with the same coats each matched the horses.

Vicki and Yarran, still approaching this regal scene noticed they were still dressed in their royal knights' armour, Swords holstered in their sheaths. As they stepped under the outreaching branches of the grand tree, a gentle breeze engulfed them. When they looked down they were now wearing beautiful royal garments with golden sashes and they each had a crown of salvation on their heads.

"Wow Vicki, you look beautiful" commented Yarran "You look like a king" remarked Vicki taking in as much of the moment as she could.

They both felt over whelmed being in the Father's Kingdom. Standing there in front of the Father and The King they could feel absolute pure love emanating all over and drenching them in it. They both dropped to their knees and said "Father, we are not worthy."

"Rise my good and faithful servants, you have served me well and we are very pleased with you." Spoke Father in such a loving voice.

The King walked over and put his hands on their shoulders. "Rise, and stand with us, you are worthy. I have made it so!"

The Kings words emanated in their spirits and they both rose to their feet and when they looked up, Eli and his entire battalion of Hosts were surrounding them in a circle encompassing them all. They were dressed in white tunics with red coloured sashes and they glistened so much that they seemed to glow. The Father stepped towards the prophets "My precious ones, my faithful son and daughter. You have done well, you have come so far and I am very proud of you both." He stretched out both his hands in front of him, palm up and two beautiful sceptres appeared.

"These I give to you my good and faithful children, you have served my kingdom well. These will gift you with kingdom wisdom and strategy." He said in a booming voice that was full of regal authority.

"Oh they are beautiful!" Explained Vicki with tears of overwhelming joy.

"Thank you Father, we are very honoured to serve you." Yarran added bowing his head.

As the prophets each took their sceptres, the sceptres rose up into the air and wrapped around each of the prophets' crowns of salvation and became a part of them. Adding to their beauty and ornately jewelled patterns.

Then Father pulled out a very official looking scroll from inside his sleeve. It had markings all over it and was encircled with a red ribbon which was fixed with a wax seal.

The scroll, like everything in Father's kingdom seemed to be alive. Father handed it to The King, who then broke the seal, held it out in front of him and let it go. The scroll hanging in mid-air unrolled itself and read out loud the message it contained.

"My faithful prophetess, you are to go to a land far from your land. You are to go to America. There you are to go to a place called the Streams of Elijah where you will meet a man named Steve, he will lead you to my prophet Jonathan who will help you in bringing my next mountain back into kingdom reign. My prophetess, Katelyn, you will meet at Paul's tent and she will go with you as well. Together you will all travel to Mount Iilannee. The creative mountain and you shall have victory."

"My Faithful prophet Yarran, I have given you an anointing for your Nation of Australia, you will stay there and guard my creation against the cruel cull orders that have been issued by the wicked. You will Prophecy to the leaders in your Nation and you will lead them into the light, making way for victory on mount Dominion. You shall be victorious."

With that the scroll rolled itself back up and vanished into thin air.

The King walked up to the prophets with a big smile and hugged them both. His arms seemed to be able to wrap around the whole world to Yarran and Vicki. They had never felt more love or joy than in that moment in The King's embrace. When He released his arms from around the prophets, He tapped Yarran's shoulder and with a big grin announced, "Now time for cake!" As he rubbed his hands together looking forward to a piece of chocolate cake.

Cheers of agreement came from the entire battalion of Hosts as they discussed who will eat the biggest piece, Eli or The King. Laughing at the thought of those two loving cake so much.

The next morning dawn broke earlier than it had in years prior due to all the dark clouds that covered the skies being gone. "Have to get used to how bright the sun is again." Joked Yarran as they packed up camp.

It was an uneventful ride back down the mountain and as it so often does on long trips, heading home seemed much quicker than getting there. The prophets parted company at the lower clearing agreeing to go home and rest up, and they would meet up at Paul's tent on Sunday morning.

Sunday morning soon came around and as arranged both Vicki and Yarran rose early to prepare the horses for the ride to the field where Paul's tent would be.

The ride there was bitter sweet for Vicki, she was a little sad that Yarran would not be with her on her next mission. But she was excited to meet Katelyn and for the adventure ahead.

As she drew near the field she could see Paul's Ute, James and Daf's car and Prophet grazing under a shady tree with Preacher lying at the base. She quickly rode over and let Rhema and Logos join them. Vicki hurried in to meet up with everyone. At the end of the teaching, Paul called for anyone who didn't know The King and would like to know him and become part of His kingdom, to come up the front.

Daf, James and their three boys were among the first to go up. Afterwards Daf gave her amazing testimony of all that had happened leading up to this moment. The entire tent was silent as she spoke, the crowd hung on every amazing word.

After she had finished, seven more entire families came up the front to meet The King. When the meeting was over the crowd gathered outside broken off into groups, everyone was excited and talking about Daf's testimony and their own experiences.

Vicki stood with Yarran, Siah, Mal, Daf, James and their family. Talking with Paul who was very excited to hear all that had been sparked by that very first chance meeting that he had with Vicki on the side of the road. This did not escape the prophets and they thanked him for his obedience to The King.

Vicki couldn't help wondering though, she was supposed to meet Katelyn but had not found her yet. Vicki's eyes scanned the crowd, she glanced over at the horses and noticed a new horse grazing with Rhema and Prophet. It was a beautiful dappled mahogany bay with four even white socks. A very nice looking horse but then, she saw a very familiar white marking on its forehead. Vicki laughed, she knew this must be Katelyn's horse, but where is Katelyn? She wondered.

There was a light tap on Vicki's shoulder, she turned to see a pretty girl with big blue eyes and long dark curly locks of hair, smiling at Vicki. "Hi, would you by any chance be Vicki?" she asked shyly.

"Yes, you must be Katelyn." Vicki responded.

"Yes, that's me." Katelyn said relieved she had found the right person.

"Oh fantastic, we have so much to talk about. You can stay at my place if you like, come on I will introduce to everyone here." Vicki introduced Katelyn to the group and after chatting for a good while, it was time to go home.

Vicki grabbed Katelyn by the arm and almost dragged her in the direction of the horses saying. "Ok now I have to meet your gorgeous horse, tell me all about him."

"Ok, well firstly he is a she, she is a mare and her name is Shekinah, she is an Egyptian Anglo Arab." Answered Katelyn laughing at Vicki's enthusiasm.

"Well at some stage you're going to have to let me have a ride, she is just beautiful."

Yarran and Vicki then introduced Katelyn to Rhema, Logos, Prophet and Preacher. Katelyn was fascinated with Prophet as she had never been so close to a brumby before, or a dingo. She wanted to learn more about them, so Yarran arranged to take her and show her the wild brumby herds in the area the next day. Kate was very excited for this, so was Vicki.

"Ok, well we better make a move, I'm starving." Said Vicki.

"You are always starving, I don't know where you put it." Laughed Yarran.

"Alright, I will meet you both at the creek tomorrow at nine in the morning. See you then!" Said Yarran as he climbed onto Prophet.

"Oh wait, I forgot, there is one more introduction I have to make." Said Katelyn as she raised her arm and whistled. There was a shriek from above them and a huge beautiful wedge tailed eagle came down and landed on Kate's arm.

"This is Glory, my eagle." She announced.

Yarran was open mouthed and managed to get out. "Super cool!"

Saving the Second Kingdom

Vicki, too was gaping, "wow! I love her!" Is all she could manage, shaking her head at how awesome The Father is!

The prophets said their goodbyes again agreeing to meet in the morning. Yarran mounted Prophet and rode off in the direction of home. The two girls rode off heading for Vicki's place. They chatted the whole way home. Vicki was so thankful to her Father for sending Katelyn to help her as she just knew they would be lifelong friends.

To the Reader

If you are being hurt or bullied in any way, please know that this story maybe fiction but The Lord -The king in these pages is very real. You are not alone, He loves you more than anything, and this book being in your hands could be The Lord reaching out to help you.

If you would like to be like Vicki and Yarran, you can be. You can have the power to speak Victory and life into everything happening in your life. All you have to do is invite Him into your heart and your life and BELIEVE!

Just say this simple prayer out loud if you can,

Dear Jesus,

I am a sinner, I am so sorry for all my sins and I ask you now to forgive me. I believe, you suffered and died on the cross and you rose again to pay for my sins. Please come into my heart and my life and help me to live in your love and Grace. Holy Spirit please live in my heart.

Thank you Jesus, Amen.

Pray for the ones hurting you and forgive them, trust that The Lord will step in and turn things around, keep believing in faith.

If you would like to invite your host army to help you go back to page 20 and speak the invitation Vicki spoke. It's real!

Glossary

Absurd	Very silly or ridiculous.
Agenda	A list or plan of things to be done.
Algorithm	Is a set of commands for a computer to perform calculations or other Problem Solving calculations
Amplified	To increase sound/ volume or to enlarge upon or add detail too.
Announcement	Officially giving information about something.
Anointed	Formally chosen officially to do an important job.
Arsenal	A store or collection of weapons
Atmosphere	The tone or mood (feeling) of a place or situation.
Atrocities	Very wicked or cruel acts.
Brumby	A feral / wild horse in Australia
Calamity	An event causing great and often sudden damage or distress
Callousness	Not caring about others
Censorship	Is a ban or blackout on words, pictures or ideas that are deemed as offensive
Ceremoniously	To observe the formal and correct way
Conscience	A persons moral sense of right and wrong

Conspiracy	The act of secretly planning with other people to do or say something bad or illegal
Conviction	A firmly held belief or opinion
Corrupt	To act dishonestly in return for money or personal gain
Cull	To reduce the population / numbers of (a wild animal) by hunting and killing them
Cylinder	A solid or hollow tube shape with long sides and two circle ends
Deception	The act of hiding the truth especially to take advantage of
Deity	A god or goddess
Deployment	Movement of soldiers or equipment
Desolate	Barron, empty or laid waste
Destiny	Something appointed and often suggests a great or noble cause
Devastation	Great destruction or damage
Dingo	A wild dog native to Australia
Disfigured	Spoiled the look of something or someone especially the face
Dominion	Control over a place or people
Ecclesia	A particular body of faithful people
Elated	Extremely happy
Encompassing	Forming a circle around something
Entities	A thing with distinct and independent existence
Extravagant	Spending or giving much more than is needed or expected
Gemmologist	One who studies gem stones

Headstock	The top of a guitar neck where the strings attach to the tuning keys
Imminent	About to happen
Independently	Not taking help or money from other people.
Indicative	A sign that something is true, exists or is likely
Interjected	To say something that interrupts someone who is speaking or thinking
Intimidating	Making you feel frightened or nervous
Jeopardy	Danger or failure
Legions	A division of 3,000 to 6,000 men / soldiers
Loathed	Intense dislike or disgust for something
Logos	The written word or word In action
Lord Sabaoth	Lord of Host Armies- The Holy Spirit
Mantle	Represents God giving us power and an assignment or job to do
Narrative	A story or description of events
Ornate	Very decorated
Pronounced	To say something in a certain way
Pursue	To follow or chase someone or something
Revelation	The act of making divine truth known
Rhema	(Ray-Mah) The spoken word
Righteousness	Acting in agreement with devine or moral law. Free from guilt or sin
Scenario	To describe what could possibly happen, a written description such as a story
Stealth	To move in a quiet way so as not to be seen or heard
Ushered	To show or guide

www.ingramcontent.com/pod-product-compliance
Lightning Source LLC
Chambersburg PA
CBHW040542170726
48295CB00012B/565